EMERGENCY

EMERGENCY

A PASTORAL NOVEL

DAISY HILDYARD

ASTRA HOUSE Λ NEW YORK

Originally published as *Emergency* by Fitzcarraldo Editions in Great
Britain, 2022.

For information about permission to reproduce selections from this book,
please contact permissions@astrahouse.com.

Astra House
A Division of Astra Publishing House
astrahouse.com
Printed in the United States of America

Library of Congress Cataloging-in-Publication Data
Names: Hildyard, Daisy, 1984– author.
Title: Emergency : a pastoral novel / by Daisy Hildyard.
Description: First edition. | New York : Astra House, 2022. |
Summary: "Our narrator is stuck at home alone under lockdown, where
she remembers her 1990s childhood in rural Yorkshire. The ecological
phenomena that start in her own backyard interconnect and spread out
from China to Nicaragua as pesticides circulate, money flows around the
planet, and bodies feel the force of distant power"—Provided by publisher.
Identifiers: LCCN 2022001562 (print) | LCCN 2022001563 (ebook) |
ISBN 9781662601477 (hardcover) | ISBN 9781662601484 (epub)
Subjects: LCGFT: Novels.
Classification: LCC PR6008.I396 E44 2022 (print) | LCC PR6008.I396
(ebook) | DDC 823/.92—dc23/eng/20220125
LC record available at https://lccn.loc.gov/2022001562
LC ebook record available at https://lccn.loc.gov/2022001563

First edition
10 9 8 7 6 5 4 3 2 1

Design by Richard Oriolo
The text is set in Arno Pro.
The titles are set in Avenir Heavy.

EMERGENCY

ONE SPRING EVENING, when I was old enough to be outside and alone, I was sitting above the quarry on the edge of the village when I saw a panel of clay drop away from the facing vertical side and fall into a pool of water. Behind it the interior of an animal's burrow was revealed in relief, like a bombed house with one wall removed. Inside, instead of wallpaper or dangling wires, there was one globe-shaped hollow lined with fluff and leaf mold, and passages leading from it which all ran through the roots of the turf, with one exception: the long tunnel which dropped down into the earth, then turned at an angle, in a stretched V-shape, and began to rise again. Within the passage, heading upward, there was a small animal—brown and furry, whether it was a mouse, a shrew, or a vole, I couldn't see.

Parallel to this creature, high above the pool of water on the quarry bed, there was a female kestrel, floating. The two creatures were at eye level with one another. The kestrel tilted and allowed herself to rise, just a little faster than the animal. Then the animal disappeared from my view, coming up through the ground; meanwhile the kestrel continued to ascend toward the clouds until, abruptly, she stopped. She stopped absolutely—as though somebody had pressed pause. Only the way her position varied very slightly, tilting one way and then another, showed that she was holding herself against a current.

Holding my gaze on her I rose slowly and as smoothly as I could, and skirted along the track that ran around the quarry at the top, taking care to make no sudden movement and to give the bird a wide berth so that she didn't flit. She must have been able to see me. She didn't move.

From the track I could see the animal again—a large vole, male, hiding under a clump of dead turf that overhung the track. He wasn't in the kestrel's eyeline. We all waited to find out who would move first. There was a clear bronze early evening light and a cold breeze. The grasses flickered. Then the vole made a sudden break, dashing into the open and stopping in the middle of the wheel-rut, right where he was most exposed. There was an island of grass in the middle of the track, and taller grasses across the field all around—this was the only area that was bald and open, and the only place the vole could look so dark and substantial against the beige dust. I stood at the edge of the track like a tree. He was almost at my feet.

The kestrel allowed her equilibrium to be disturbed. She tipped her body, carved a line in the air, and came to hover directly above the vole. Low sunlight projected her shadow away from her so that it fell beyond his horizon. Still the vole remained in the same place. I could see him intimately now—his features were precise and miniature: acorn-cup ears, thread-fine whiskers radiating in all directions, and tiny hand-shaped feet. His whole body was vibrating violently. He seemed unable to move. The kestrel had paused again and my gaze moved up and down, drawing a direct line between them, like a lift between two floors of a building. I felt a sense of love arise inside me, as huge and widespread as the vole was small and specific, and it occurred to me that I could rescue him.

I knew what this would mean because I'd done it before. When the huge black rabbit who lived in a run in our garden had a nest full of babies, my parents had told me not to touch them. I sat outside the hutch and waited for them to be revealed when their mother rolled aside—tiny pink squirming things which were in the process of becoming, from day to day, delicate versions of their parents. When they were a week or so old, skin still visible through a sheen of black fur, my mother explained why I wasn't to touch them: the rabbit would eat her babies if they had a strange smell on them. I held my hands in front of my face but they didn't smell like anything except, faintly, soap. My mother left and I stayed watching the rabbits for a while. Then I put one in my pocket, closed the lid of the hutch at the end of the run, and ran down the drive, along the street, and into Clare's garden. Clare wasn't there, but Nic was sitting on the back step with a mug of tea and a biscuit, one cigarette waiting beside her on the warm brick. She was always there, waiting like that when Clare came home from school. I closed the gate and approached, warily, up the path, until I was in front of her, waiting for a sign that she had recognized me, but she wasn't much interested in my presence—she was still looking over my shoulder. I glanced behind me but there was nothing there, only the sun setting over the fields and the quarry. There was a small yellowish scar below the outer edge of one of her eyes which very slightly affected its shape, so there was always something unusual about her face, but in that moment she was looking toward the sun and her brown iris seemed to have been set on fire, melting diamonds of golds and oranges wheeling around the rim, which gave her a blind, illuminated fierceness, and I felt afraid of her. Then it passed and I said, "Hi, is Clare playing?"

Nic didn't say hello or speak in the indulgent but dishonest tone that adults usually used when speaking to me at that time in my life. Distractedly, still looking with disturbing directness into the sun, she told me that Clare wasn't yet home because she had gone to her grandmother's house after school. Adam was inside, watching a cartoon, if I wanted to wait.

In the front room Adam was cross-legged on the floor very close to the television, having bricked himself into a low wall of wooden blocks. I kneeled behind him and we sat quietly together to watch a squirrel being electrocuted, then guillotined, having its head glued back on, having its eyes plucked out, and being run over by a truck, until Nic opened the curtains, turned down the sound, and asked me whether I wanted to stay for tea, and I said yes. She asked me whether my parents would mind and I didn't reply. Then there was a thump.

Clare's schoolbag was on the mat where the post would land, and Clare silhouetted behind it in the open doorway.

"Why is there a ladder on the side of the house?" she announced.

Nic told Clare that her dad was fixing a leak in the guttering.

"Adam," said Clare. "Would you like to go up that ladder?"

Adam knocked down his barricade and toddled over to Clare, who took his hand. They went outside and I followed.

Clare and I stood at the bottom of the ladder, holding it steady while Adam slowly climbed. The ladder did not seem to be going anywhere—it didn't reach the roof, and that side of the house had only one small frosted window high up. Between the red bricks the mortar was covered over by mosses which traced out a regular but complicated shape, a dark green maze. Down here, near the ground, the mosses were plush, with threads like yellow walking sticks

sticking out of their surfaces. Looking at their still, shadowy softness, I felt a deep calm feeling drop through me. On the upper part
of the wall above me, where full sun hit the brick, they had dried to a
cracked pale color but on the other side, above Clare's head, these
corpses had come to life. It wasn't a miracle: the leak in the guttering, which I couldn't see, was revealed by a widening spill of water
down the side of the house. This had woken up the mosses who had
advanced out over the brick, thickening and growing emerald and
black as they wettened, like waterweed. Even at that age, I knew it
wasn't ideal for the wall. I realized that the sense of stillness that the
mosses opened up inside me, which I experienced as a feeling, was
in fact a pace—we were out of step. I moved through mornings and
weekends, months and dinners, while the mosses, somewhere
beyond my time frame, moved through their alien periods of torpor
and spreading.

When I turned away from the wall Clare's head was almost
touching mine. Her eyes were much darker than her mother's,
almost black. I must have stared open-mouthed because she dropped
her jaw like an idiot. I felt something moving inside my pocket.

"Oh," I said. "Look."

I stepped away from the ladder and took the tiny rabbit out of
my pocket. Holding it in my curled fist, my fingers formed a loose
tunnel around it. Suddenly I felt unwilling to reveal it. Its silk fur
was damp and pricklier than before, either from the sweat inside my
hands or from its own piss. Clare raised her eyebrows at my hesitation, and this made my hand open like a flower, without any
conscious will. The rabbit's ears lay flat. They were thin and fuzzy,
like new leaves when they first push out of the bud.

Clare said, "Put it back or it will die."

I told her that I was taking care of it and Clare groaned and rolled her eyes, extravagantly reasonable, and told me that I would learn the hard way.

A sharp voice came from high above us: "Clare, get your brother down or you'll crack his head open."

I looked up. The bathroom window was tilted open like a letter-box. I couldn't see Nic.

We ignored her. Clare leaned one arm loosely against the base of the ladder, ready to break Adam's fall, but he was safe, still climbing with dimpled gripping hands and flat feet. He climbed and climbed until he reached the face of the wall. Then I went home and put the rabbit back. My mother said I couldn't go to Clare's for tea, she'd already made something for me.

The following day I went to see the rabbits and the mother was alone in her run. She was truly a big rabbit. I watched her for a while. She seemed calm, nibbling dandelion leaves, and I felt a sense of affinity with her because we had done it together, destroyed the babies with our colossal care. Even today, she seems to me very human in the way her principles forced her to self-destruct, and in the scale of her appetite, which far exceeded what she needed to survive—those dandelion leaves. I don't mean that the rabbit was much like a person, more that principles and will, among most other qualities (memory, love), are not exclusively human traits by any reasonable definition. All creatures have character.

When I started going to school I had to walk home from the school bus and this meant that I passed Grace and Matthew's unfenced front garden where their dog Soldier lived. I was afraid of Soldier because she ran out barking excitedly whenever a person passed by on foot and she was, to me, huge—she had a syrup-colored coat which flowed out behind her as she galloped down the sloping garden. She was old, her jaw wrinkled and slackening to reveal the pointed back teeth. The scary thing was her most vulnerable place, her underbelly, which was bald and mottled brown and purple, with swollen teats. Grace and Matthew, who were kind to me, said that she was only playing, and it was true that she never jumped onto the pavement, or came onto our side of the front garden—there was no fenced division and she could easily have done it. But in spite of her regard for these boundaries, I was troubled by a vision I had of being pinned down under Soldier's body with the bald patch obscenely in contact with my own stomach, looking up into the mouth which was threaded with lines of drool and hanging open in its slack way above my face. This image was vivid to me in a way that made it unimportant as to whether I had dreamed or remembered it. And so I started turning right just before I reached our road and walking around the block, anti-clockwise, to come at my house from the other side without passing Soldier.

Instead I passed Alice's house, at the back of the village, and its tree which had a hollow where Clare and I hid things. It was a thing I'd read about in a library book and the story flowed into my reality and my real life leaked back into the story. My idea, which I'd taken from a book about children whose parents were separated, was that Clare and I could leave messages or objects for one another in a secret location. Clare decided on the tree. She was older than me and decisions were her strong point. When she told me, decisively, that we would use the witch tree, I knew that she was talking about the ash tree which grew out of the very back corner by Alice Gray's house, and that Clare's name for it was the right name. The ash would have been taken down if it had been on any other property— you couldn't pass it without feeling its threatening glamour, the tree was somehow exuberant even though it was so very dead. It grew out of the loose stone wall which bulged and sagged on either side of the fat trunk, and its topmost twigs went higher than the buildings, the end of its branches twisted into the sky in paused spasms, the wood blackened and rotting. There were tiny white mushrooms and larger apricot-colored mushrooms on the tree all year round, and the spores and enzymes that were engaged in the long process of digesting the wood gave the whole tree a sodden look, so that its deadness was irradiated with living.

People said that Alice was a witch, though she wasn't that old. One side of her body was out of sync with the other—her mouth dropped down at one edge and the corresponding leg dragged. Among the children it was understood that she had been pulling a face when the wind changed. She had short hair and round glasses and she looked like a small man, dressed in a long cloth waistcoat and combat trousers. We gravitated toward her door when we played knock-and-run. It was one of those miniature persecutions that children rehearse, with an instinct for victimizing difference, though it was also because we knew we'd get a response: Alice never went out. She was always in her kitchen, right beside the back door, so she was always available.

The hollow was perfect: a small opening near the base of the trunk in which, if I reached my hand, I could feel a dry, football-sized cavity with a mealy floor. I passed it after school every day and sometimes Clare would leave an object inside for me, things that seem like nothing now—a lip balm or a postcard. Then there was the day when I saw a slice of cake on the low back wall of the farm, right under the branches of our dead tree. I lifted the cake and it was light, the kind of chocolate cake which doesn't contain any actual chocolate, and still warm, the icing turning to liquid against my fingertips. It smelled good. I placed it back carefully on the wall, in the same place. The next day it was gone. I wondered if I had imagined it but there were crumbs above our hollow. Perhaps Clare had left it for me.

When I asked her, later, playing in her garden, she widened her eyes and denied it.

"Not me," she said, shaking her head. "I wonder what on earth it could have been." Then she ran away from me. "Come here," she called from the bottom of the jungle gym. "Do this."

I went, obedient, and crossed the monkey bars well enough until I reached the final rung, which came away in my hand, dropping me seven feet onto the grass. I stood up, experimentally moving my fingers, and Clare laughed with deep pleasure. She had a manly, guffawing laugh which took over the trunk of her body, which made me laugh with her and at her at the same time, which made us both laugh harder.

It occurred to me then that the ash tree itself had made the cake, or consumed it. The tree, like all the things that rampaged on its dead body, like Soldier, like the rabbits, like the moss on the side of Clare's house, like the kestrel and the vole—they were all part of my community, as I then thought of it, at least as much as myself or Nic or Alice. Though our village was inside this community, the community went beyond the village. As I saw it, the whole area for miles around was part of the wood: the village, the river, the farms, the wild animals, the quarry, the stately home, the housing estate, the bacon factory, the ruined abbey—they were all surrounded and overrun by woodland which was patchily logged by the Forestry Commission, so that it was hard to identify the place where it ended or began; it ran through all these things, and all these things moved through the wood in their different ways. Birch Wood, it was called, though the name was an old one and there were no birch trees there in my lifetime. We had a silver birch in our garden so I could imagine the birch forest which used to inhabit the site, pale glowing ghost trees stretching to the horizon—but when I was there it was mostly cherry and ash and a few perfect squares of pine plantation, running to the edge of the quarry where the ground dropped.

I used to sit at the top of that cliff for long stretches of time because I liked the view—the quarry was many different colors and they were all gentle, layered pale browns and chalks. The way the earth had been scooped out meant that I could look down on a portion of sky which was made visible in the negative: a bowl of birds soaring down below my feet. Sand martins made their homes in the sides and flew out into the quarry to catch insects; falcons came to hunt the sand martins, and I came to watch them all because there wasn't anything better to do. That was how I was there to see the kestrel hunting the vole, which was how I came to know about the water in the quarry before the others.

I was standing and waiting for the vole or the kestrel to move and something clicked. It was physical and visual, like a camera finding focus. The V-shaped tunnel, going down, and then veering back toward the surface, literally spelled out to me the fact that the vole had hit water—that water was rising through the earth, high up the sides of the quarry. I had seen the panel of clay landing in a pool of water on the quarry bed. But the picture bobbed meaninglessly among the debris of what feels like a tidal wave of random information that crashes over me every moment. I like to think that I would go mad if I tuned in to everything, all the time, the squirrel's heartbeat or the roar of growing grass, but this is most likely a lie—realistically, the business of relentlessly prioritizing and deleting the details of the world is the mad element. There shouldn't have been a pool of water on the quarry bed.

The quarry had flooded, just a little, years earlier, but since then it had been drained because the flooding had caused problems. The animals who had made their homes in and around the quarry began to move, which put pressure on the territories. Humans were no exception. Most adults in the area were employed by the quarry or the bacon factory, and the gardens on my street were built right out up to the patch of scrubby edgeland I was standing on.

Our quarry produced gravel which was sent all over the world. The requirements of Norwegian motorways and new cities in China determined the shape of the quarry and the size of the space it left, though the relationship went in both directions, in every direction. Stones, single hairs, and skin flakes from the workers' bodies and fragments of rubber from the old tires of the quarry's two vehicles traveled the globe. The place was dynamited apart and distributed throughout the world in vanishingly small splinters and particles. As a child I watched it go but I couldn't see where it went. As an adult I have a stronger but still slight understanding of how my resources reach me, or how my life extends into the dams, logging operations, fulfilment centers, makeshift mining towns, oilfields, or containment facilities on which my daily life depends. These resources, like my quarry, are sited not only where they will be cheap, but also where they will be largely unseen by human eyes.

I never went inside the pigsties but they were impossible to ignore because they were on the horizon and the lights never went off—the pigs lived in perpetual strip-lit daytime. Ann's mom said it made them more eager to die. Ann's mom, sitting in a plastic chair in her back garden with her head tipped back to catch the remaining UV, once told Ann and her sisters and me the story of her working day, how she stood, wearing waders, for five hours at a time in a windowless, high-walled room with a hole in the floor. Cleaned pig corpses, suspended over her head on a wire track, were pulled into the middle of the room. Their cavities would open down a central line and their insides landed in front of her. She had a broom with a hose running through it that was used to clear blood and heaps of offal into a chute toward the part of the factory that produced the sausage meat.

I enjoyed this story not so much for the gore as for the way Ann's mom shrugged, cool, when we children expressed our horror, and told us that the worst thing was the boredom. She was a tiny woman with faded roses tattooed along one arm and shoulder, red hennaed hair, three young daughters, a nineteen-year-old boyfriend, and a talent for peaceful enjoyment which she spread around her house and garden—a part of me wants to say that she was living her best life, but that would be glib. When she told us stories about her job she began to open up some basic understanding of the human landscape in my mind. I could see an unequal difference in the space between the work my parents did (my father was working on short-term contracts at universities and colleges, and as a painter and decorator; my mother was a supply teacher) and the things Ann's mother went out to do. There was another distinction between the unsteady work my parents did and the real teachers or doctors, who had cars and took holidays. Farming, which my grandmother did nearby, was altogether a different way to be. I would have struggled to explain how these things related to one another with any consistency.

The first time it was known that the quarry was flooding, the local councillor called a meeting in the community center. It was not well attended. There was no great sense of urgency, perhaps because the quarry was operating as usual, only with a big puddle on one side. At the community meeting the conversation moved instead toward the fox problem. It was breeding season and foxes were fucking and feuding in our gardens over territory. When they cried they sounded tortured, as though they were experiencing some psychological horror that was worse than any physical pain. Sometimes they triggered the security light that Matthew and Grace had set up above their back door, and my bedroom was immersed in a reflected white glare. I kneeled up in bed to look out of my window just in time to spy back legs and long tails flowing out of the pool of light and into the tattered shadow around the edges. The stainless-steel dustbin lid would drop, clang, then roll in a long curve, ringing deeply. It sounded merry, like it found the whole situation a laugh.

I saw the foxes in my own garden just once. It was disturbing. They were dancing. Kneeling on my bed I could see two foxes close to the back wall of my house in the open part of the concrete yard. One fox was very small. She flattened herself down onto the ground, hip bones making small hills in her flank. The other fox was huge and he was facing her. He had a broad face, a thick, fluffy neck, and a wide tail with a white tag. Slowly, as the small fox united herself with the ground, the large fox reared and rose until he was standing on his hind legs, and then he stepped from foot to foot, his front paws hanging in the air, his long body not quite stable—he heeled from one side to the other, just catching himself at either extreme. This went on for minutes. The small fox watched. I watched. And then I noticed another fox, a little way back, face turned intently toward the pair of them from behind a patch of the ivy which grew thickly on the fence. I could see the third fox's narrow head angling toward the dancer, then toward the one he was dancing for. I realized that she wasn't watching them, she was turning to catch their scent.

I got out of bed and went downstairs to tell my parents but it was later than I'd thought. Nobody was awake and the lights were out. When I tiptoed into the middle of the darkened room something stirred on the sofa. My mother sat up and pushed away blankets. I halted in front of her. She told me that there had been an argument. "Things will be normal in the morning."

I noticed nothing unusual in the morning and I didn't give it much thought. But when I went with my father to the community meeting about the quarry I wasn't surprised by the fact that those who attended argued over what to do about the foxes. Commuters wanted to accommodate them and farmers wanted to shoot them—one farmer said that he had lost several valuable Christmas geese to a huge dog fox which he had shot the previous weekend, and the bullet had gotten sucked into the fox's hide.

At the end of the meeting the principal from my school stood up and suggested that the quarry should be decommissioned and returned to nature. This was happening, she said, with the slag heaps from the closed mines, which were being given to local wildlife trusts. She made the quarry sound like an object which our community had purchased, though it didn't suit us. Sparsely dispersed throughout the community hall, the group responded evasively. There were tiny, noncommittal noises in the backs of throats. Fractional nods, just to register that she was audible. These days I would say that her proposal was a good idea.

There were two classes in my school, with three year-groups in the lower class (mine) and four in the upper. Ms. Carr taught top class and so she had a special aura to those of us in lower class. She held assembly, made announcements, and came into our classroom only on exceptional occasions, like the spring day when our usual teacher, Mrs. Hepton, vanished at dinnertime. Beside the teacher's desk, occupying the space where our nature table had been, there was a wheeled cafeteria cook's cart, and Ms. Carr stood in front of it. She told us to practice our spelling in silence. She left the room and closed the door.

Heads lifted and we looked around at one another. The classroom was an environment of its time: the boys all had curtains or shaved heads; the girls wore high ponytails like fountains, two strands of hair released at the front, and the tiny plastic trolls on their desks had received the same treatment, neon hair bunched in tiny scrunchies. These silent, uniformed heads, male, female, troll, all seemed to be listening to Ms. Carr's soles sticking on the linoleum as she walked across the corridor, opened the door to her own classroom, took a reading of the quality of quiet inside, and then closed it again. When she reappeared in front of us our interest in her waned and we looked down at our desks again.

The desks came from a different era: old, wooden, lidded, with inkwells and hollow insides that were regularly inspected to ensure that all books were stored regularly, in ascending order of size, and perhaps also to show each child that there was no private space. I must have spent many weeks in total staring into mine, and before me another child, and before that another, each one of us working with our faces so close to the surface that our breath warmed the wood, which exhaled its own dry scent, so oppressively close that we could see an irregular elongation in the patterns where the tree had swollen rapidly through a wet spring sometime in the nineteenth century, and the place on the surface where the carpenter, a few years later, had shifted his plane to a different angle, and the place beneath the loose hinge where somebody, more recently, had drawn a tiny pair of breasts.

A few minutes after Ms. Carr's return a subtle shift of attention moved within the line of students who were sitting closest to the window. Outside Mrs. Hepton was opening the double gates to the road. She walked backward onto the grass so that a van could reverse into the playground. A man climbed out and opened the doors at the back of the van so that they mirrored the gates to the playground: two pairs of wings spread wide.

Inside the van there was a very large cardboard box. Our teacher and the man lifted it out and placed it on the ground behind the van. There were two smaller boxes behind it. I closed my eyes and listened. A car passed through the village. Sparrows squabbled on the concrete. Clare, who was sitting in the desk in front of me, scribbled her pen back and forth to obliterate something she had written. There was a thud in the corridor and somebody swore, then apologized. I opened my eyes to look at Clare, Clare turned around and widened her eyes at me. Nobody dared to laugh. Then at last the door burst open and the boxes were brought in, one by one, and placed in front of our trolley. Each one was taller than a child. I could see, from the way they were carried, that they were heavy and valuable.

After the man had gone Ms. Carr and Mrs. Hepton stood together at the front of the room between their pupils and the huge boxes. Ms. Carr tall, remote, and serene; Mrs. Hepton short. Both wore huge plastic-framed spectacles and had tightly curled set hair, but down on the ground their differences were undeniable: Mrs. Hepton's orthopedic sandals revealed large toes webbed by flesh-colored tights. Ms. Carr's low-heeled shoes were white, matching her white artificial silk skirt and t-shirt: she floated above her colleague, high and triumphant—she looked like a calla lily, a white flame, a victor. Her fingers twirled with nervous excitement which made the smeary gold on her rings flash, as she announced that our posters and fundraising fêtes had been successful. She had purchased the school a computer. In the future, she told us with her voice shaking very slightly, we would all work on computers. Every word we wrote would be word-processed.

As she spoke she caught our eyes, one by one—it felt uncomfortable, I could see that it was a deliberate effect. Meanwhile Mrs. Hepton raised her eyes and fixed them grimly on the clock at the back of the room. It was Mrs. Hepton who had, patiently and against the odds, taught each one of us to read and to write with a sharpened HB pencil, in lowercase. Once we had mastered this, beginning again at "a," we learned to connect the letters, until eventually, in ones and twos, we were presented with a pen when—*and only when*—the joined-up handwriting merited ink. A few children were never awarded pens and Mrs. Hepton did nothing to take the edge off their shame: shame was elemental to her teaching, together with chanting, tidiness, obedience, and silence.

As we unpacked the computer Mrs. Hepton remarked on how much space it took up and the fact that it occupied the nature table's area. She wondered aloud why it was not placed in Miss Carr's classroom. Ms. Carr replied that the nature table could be moved into the back corner and that her own class already had a greater number of students within a smaller room. She no longer corrected the Miss.

When the computer was assembled on the trolley it stood higher than the teacher's desk. It was browned white, the color of the stone from the local quarry, and I wonder now why the plastic was chosen in that particular shade, as though the designers wanted their machine to represent something geological—the mine or quarry from which its internal minerals had been unpacked before they were processed, bestowed with new forms of intelligence, and then closed away again within the plastic shell. We opened the box with curiosity and caution, as though it was a live animal, gaining confidence as the computer emerged from its den of cardboard, polyethylene slips, and polystyrene bows. One child drew a fingernail across the grainy surface of the monitor's casing and it made a low, rasping noise. Ms. Carr flinched.

Then the hard drive, the monitor, the removable disk drives, and the keyboard were in place, and we were left with a snake's nest of wires and cables with plugs of different shapes at the end of them. John Green, one of those who had not yet earned a pen, and who skipped school if his dad was doing something interesting on the farm, plumped down on the floor behind the trolley with a look of happy concentration on his face, connecting machine to wire, wire to machine. Eventually he stood and gave the nod. Ms. Carr pushed the largest plug into the wall and flicked the switch beside the socket, and nothing happened.

"It doesn't work," said Mrs. Hepton.

Ms. Carr frowned.

"This is where you switch it on," said John, allowing himself the suggestion of a smile. He pressed the button.

There was a feeling of a sudden swelling and filling, as though a hot wind was gusting into the room, when the fans inside the machine first breathed. After a short time, the cursor appeared with a bleep, blinking.

The school computer didn't have an internet connection and I did not yet know any homes with a desktop monitor, though many of us had Sega Genesis's and Game Boys. I used to play on the computer at Clare's house on the days when the pesticide sprayers went out. She and I looked forward to these days because our mothers kept us inside and we had snacks and television and computer games in exchange for keeping quiet. When we played *Sonic* Clare was on a level so high that it seemed theoretical to me, like heaven, and she didn't even bother playing *Tetris* anymore, but when we played the game that involved shooting down airplanes, each one a rudimentary construction whose wings were ziggurats of pixels, my nervous reflexes were quicker than hers and I took down plane after plane after plane. Clare cackled with pleasure at my unnerving ability. "It's not like you." It felt good to win.

Spraying days happened mostly in late spring when the weeds came up and rain came down. Molds and mildews bloomed in the fields. Our street was a row of semi-detached houses that had been built between the wars. The four on the edge of the village, which included Clare's, faced out above the quarry. They were council-owned. The other four, including mine, were closer to the center of the village and were owned by their inhabitants. Clare's home faced the quarry and mine faced large cultivated fields, bare and sloping, whose hedges had been stripped out, where wheat and barley were rotated with broad beans. These fields caught the sun but their soil was heavy and water-retentive and so they needed pesticides in order to produce a yield. They needed them: this was one of the facts that were produced inside the world we lived in; it was necessary and therefore it had to be true.

I played deep inside these fields and so I knew its other pests well. Small shiny-coated insects crowded at the base of the hairs on an ear of barley, each cluster bulging to the size and shape of one blob on a blackberry. Grey beardy stuff that looked like cotton fluff or goose-down grew between the stalks and retained water after a rainfall. This material compounded the problem of a third pest that manifested as pinpoints of black dust that marbled the criss-crossed grains on an ear of wheat.

Even in dry weather the interior of the field was damp. If I played inside it my bare arms or legs would come out soaked and itchy with a white bumpy rash. The smell of wet barley, like washing that has been left too long in the machine, rose out of the fields on hot still days after rain, nauseatingly static. But the spraying was beautiful and I loved it—I loved the opportunity it gave me to stay inside Clare's house for hours at a time, and I admired its verve, Thomas Gray in his tractor racing up and down, flying too fast over the bumps, with ballerina skirts of vapor pouring behind him, still puffing, in fading asthmatic stutters, as he returned along the road. My mother gave a basic explanation of how this mist crept into lungs and how its tiny dots would morph into floating shapes that would then twirl through the blood. I pictured particles tumbling chaotically like Tetris blocks, which needed to be addressed swiftly and decisively if they were to slot correctly into the body.

Perhaps these stories gave Clare and me a cue: while we were inside we discovered the rush that came from hyperventilating. We would breathe rapidly until our minds spiraled off giddily and our bodies laughed without knowing why. This was not a silent game and Nic told us to keep it down. "You'll shrink your brains," she said. Then she left. I looked at Clare and Clare began to count us in again. Spraying days gave me something to respect. If the invisible air was loaded with invisible poisons, if my own bloodstream could be modeled by its tiniest contaminant component, then it was only logical to understand that the whole, infinitely detailed world, within and beyond the things that I could make sense of, was dangerous. This was not what I felt as I moved freely around the village and the wood. I had a sense of total safety and this was a function of my background—my white body and my parents' confidence gave me a relationship with that environment that ran somewhere between feeling that I belonged to it, and feeling that it belonged to me, though I did not know of any child in our community, along any of the axes that were used to identify us—rich or poor; black or white; girl or boy; beautiful or ugly; strong or weak; bright or thick— who was kept inside out of a concern for their bodily safety. I had access to the wood, the fields, and to other people's homes as though I was an element of infrastructure, piped water or electrical wiring, running under the ground, between the trees, through and within the houses with a supply of something that the inhabitants, whether through habit or deep dependence, had stopped noticing. They trusted me because I was small, indeterminate of gender, slow, and wheezily asthmatic: clearly unthreatening—in fact, barely functioning—and because I was polite. Politeness was rare in the community and though the people there, who were mostly pragmatic, did not have much time for it, they feared it: it stank of power. My parents were deeply invested in the concept of manners and I found that it was easy to gain entry to anybody else's house by thanking and pleasing the people who lived there. I was given a lot of biscuits and I drank a lot of squash. These days most of my relationships are with less pragmatic people and my politeness more frequently emerges as uncertainty in this habitat.

I remember Alice calling me into her house in springtime to stroke a lamb who was living in a dog-basket beside the fire. The lamb was not cute—there was bloody mucus trailing from its nostril and each breath made a wet, spongy sound. I over-identified, I knew what it was like to struggle for breath. Like a wild or savage animal, I was driven by a need to care for something. I took the lamb out of the basket and sat stroking it on my knee inside a deep armchair, leaning off the side into the green glazed tiles which radiated warmth back from the wall. The oven was on and the dense smell of black ginger cake was in the air. Alice spoke: "Do you ride?"

She had turned away from me, her face in shadow. I told her that I was allergic to horses but she didn't seem to hear me.

"When I was not much older than you," she said, "I had three ponies and I set up a riding school. Very good people sent their children."

She turned to face me and pronounced a long male name I didn't recognize. When I didn't respond she told me that this man was a concert pianist, and that she, Alice, had been earning quite a lot of money. Quite a lot. She bought several more ponies. But then her headmistress wrote to her father and told him that she would fail her school exams if she didn't close her riding school.

Alice laughed humorlessly and her story petered out. "So then I had too many ponies! I couldn't ride them all myself."

She had a vaguely pleased or bewildered expression which made her look holy. I supposed she was thinking about specific ponies. It was quiet in the kitchen. Then there was a loud banging on the door.

I tried to get up but I was stuck inside the armchair's collapsed seat. Alice chuckled at the sight of me as she limped over to open it. Step, drag. Step, drag. I sat back and pressed the side of my face against the hot green tiles.

There was nobody behind the door. We had both known there wouldn't be. Alice turned back to look at me and winked, and the action, which spread laboriously over her face, was all wrong.

"I'm sorry," I said. She shook her head.

"It feels different in here, doesn't it," she said. "With me."

I saw food on the wall beside my ash tree outside her house several times. After the cake there was a saucepan with a thick layer of porridge crusted on the sides and base, flapjack pieces that had crumbled, and a warm broken scone. I never touched them and never again mentioned them to Clare though I still suspected her of something, but I didn't have the imagination to see what. Then one evening I was walking past the farm and the tree when somewhere in my eyeline, along the distant edge of the wood, a patch of trees appeared to shift. It was indistinct, an uneven convulsion in an area of brown shadows. As it enlarged it separated itself from the line of trees and became a small female deer. She didn't have that elegance that most deer have, picking their way from one footstep to the next—there was a drag on her as though one side was walking in a shallow ditch. When she came closer I could see that one of her forelegs did not have a foot: the hide ended above the hoof in a clean, squarish cutoff. I couldn't see a scar.

The deer stepped out onto the road. She paused and raised her nose, then resumed her advance to the wall where she ate the cold pancake that had been left out. She took her time and showed no concern for my presence. I wondered how the deer and Alice had found one another.

Another day, in the same place, I saw a very different thing. I was walking home from school and could hear a regular smacking noise as I approached the entrance to Alice Gray's farm. There was a dull quality to the sound which made me feel sick. As I passed, I turned to look inside. Inside the yard, closer to me than I had expected, I saw Alice in profile, standing at her full height with a small axe high above her head. She was beside the huge dead ash tree. Her axe had made a dent and a small, mangled hole in the base of its soft trunk. It was the other side to my hollow. I could see that the wood was too soft to chop: the edges of the hole were frayed and crumpled. The axe fell again. The sound it made was flat, as though the surface was covered with thick leather, and the wood caved in around it, making a large circular dent in the trunk rather than splitting neatly. If the tree fell it would knock down Alice's wall and block the road, locking her neighbors in.

Alice was wearing a vest and heavy sand-colored denim trousers. There was black-grey hair in her armpits and the underside of her upper arms looked muscly and jaundiced. Her axe fell with a heavy fluid movement into the tree. The unevenness of Alice's body was not discernible in this powerful form. Each swing was straight and forceful. This was a different person to the woman who dragged her leg from the table to the dresser to fetch black molasses: this person moved smoothly, the only sign of effort the yelp that jerked out of her as the axe fell. It sounded fragmented, as though she needed to clear her throat. The trunk reluctantly split and she stood, drew her arms together, and raised them high above her head and let them fall, and she yelped again. But then she raised her axe and sent it into the trunk at shoulder height, and then she chopped again, and then again and again, so that she was making many tiny cuts in the trunk. I frowned: this would never make any difference to the tree. The wood mashed in splinters and Alice made the yelping sound again. The axe skidded down the bark almost vertically. It wasn't cutting. I couldn't see her face, only her body. The axe went down again, making soft splinters in the smashed wood. I continued to watch quietly. Her frenzy made me feel particularly still. It was a feeling I've experienced not many times, when an image *comes alive*, as people say. The face of a young man from Mali, the only person on a crowded inflatable boat who is looking directly at the camera, or the grasping hands of a woman in the background of an old picture, painted in with a few brushstrokes. Not a sense of identification but a feeling that the body you are looking at is vital because it is distinct. I don't think the ash tree could feel anything—feel, fell—but what do I know.

Suddenly Alice looked right at me. She still had her axe in her hand. It floated up toward her shoulder as we stared at one another. She said that the tree should have been taken down a long time ago. She dipped her head and I slightly bent mine, then like a pair of courting pigeons her head rose again and I quickly straightened up too. Alice's face broke down into a smile. "Come inside," she said. "I've made rolls."

The tree was still standing. She had made a mess of its bark. I checked the other side of the tree, the hollow side. Clare's side and mine. But there was nothing in the hollow and it was undamaged.

I picked up a spike of material from the mashed edge of the tree. It was warm from the friction and the interior was made of strings of wood, flexible, with that pink tinge that live wood has which soon disappears from the log's complexion. There was a knot of denser material which had come away whole, leaving a crater in one part. I smoothed my fingertips along its length and pressed the sharp point into my fingertip so that my skin dented, but the wood was too soft to cut me. The tree had been leafless for my whole life. Surely it couldn't have been alive. I looked up into its black twigs, which scratched the air very slightly. There was no wind down where I was.

When we were inside Alice seemed like her normal self. We ate warm, soft white rolls. I asked her to teach me how to bake.

"You think that's all I'm good for."

OVER TIME THE CUT AT the base of the ash tree grew a frame of black rot around its edges, and perhaps the tree tilted slightly over the wall, out over the road, but maybe it had always been like that. It didn't fall, and Clare and I continued to leave things in our hollow from time to time, before and after our usual journeys to and from school, where we spent most of our time together too. This was lucky for me because I needed Clare's protection. She seemed to know what the teacher required of us as though she had received advance instructions. When we were given paper plates and paint and told to draw our favorite food, I looked over to Clare. She drew a neat line down the middle of her plate: chips on the left, vanilla milk to the right. Hesitantly, I drew a small picture on one side of the plate and colored it in. Mrs. Hepton, pacing in clockwise rotation around the activity desk, swooped. She held up my picture vertically so that the paint began to run across the penciled outlines and trickle so that the shape drizzled over the borders and made no sense anymore. "What are you doing?" asked Mrs. Hepton. Her voice was shrill and she sounded scared.

"Do we eat mice, children? Do we eat mice in this class?"

"It is not a mouse," I said, looking in horror at the plate that I had done.

Clare looked over. She had finished her picture and was waiting with folded hands for the rest of the class to catch up. "Ha," she said. "Good one."

A mouse was not food. I did not want to explain that it was a shrew. A shrew was not food either, most likely.

"Perhaps," said Clare, "she was thinking it was food for something else. For example, a bird of prey, a sparrow hawk, a buzzard, a falcon, or an owl which eats mice and spits mouse pellets."

Mrs. Hepton asked: "Is that what you were thinking?"

I nodded. I did not say that I couldn't see why it was so useful to call some birds *birds of prey*, when each individual bird was different, and all birds were just birds. It didn't occur to me to mention the truth: I'd just felt like drawing a shrew. It was only thanks to Clare that I didn't have to explain myself. She gave me cover, like a tree which creates seclusion for some smaller, weaker, shade-loving plant, and this happened day after day after day. It didn't always help our friendship. When Mrs. Hepton asked me what my father did for a living it was Clare who obscured the uncertainty that would have betrayed me. We were doing topic work on "Work" and I didn't know what my father's true work was. He painted houses—not pictures of houses, but brick fronts and window frames. He helped on farms. On some envelopes he was addressed as a doctor. There were times when he was teaching in a prison, or a summer school, or an adult education college, and there were times when he had been let go. And yet I was aware that none of these things were truly what he *did*. This was an impression I had. It did not come from direct observation, but from conversations between my parents that I had overheard without listening to—it had to do with the tone in which they talked about these jobs, rather than the words they used.

I could feel Mrs. Hepton's attention on me. There was something she wanted to extract from me, something she needed to identify. Then Clare put up her hand, inhaling deep into her ribcage as though she was almost bursting in her desperation to announce: "*My* dad works at the quarry and my mum just sits around watching Sky."

Mrs. Hepton turned, the corners of her mouth lifting. "Who told you that?"

"My nana told me," said Clare, "and my dad told me." She shrugged. "Now I'm telling you."

The bell rang.

In the playground Clare walked over to the hedge and selected one of the sharp white stones that lay under it. She used this stone to draw a line on the tarmac—the beginnings of goalposts or hopscotch. I crouched over Clare as she crouched to draw. She straightened up and I followed suit. She told me to tell her the truth about my parents and I told her that my father was a doctor.

Then Clare took my arm in her hands tenderly. Gently, she turned it over to expose the paler underside between elbow and wrist. With intensifying pressure she scraped the sharp edge of her stone along this part of my arm. The stone was hot from friction with the tarmac. A layer of my skin peeled off like Saran Wrap, so thin that it took a moment for the blood to rise through to the surface. Then Clare knocked the stone against my head, not hard enough to knock me over, but hard enough to make me feel it as a cobble inside my head knocking against the insides of the skull walls. When I touched the side of my head there was blood on the pad of my finger. Orangey.

Clare then stood with her arms out as if she was pretending to be an airplane, her fist balled too tightly around the stone. The smooth skin of her hands had creamy patches on the knuckles, with the force she had bunched up. Her eyes were red and fierce. "You're full of shit," she said. "Remember that we're best friends."

Every day we traveled out together, Clare and I, and every day we walked home from the school bus until I turned off to avoid Soldier, who lived between the two of us on the short street. Our two homes were almost identical, as buildings seen from the outside, but on the inside, Clare's home was the place where I wanted to live. My house was haunted, not by ghosts exactly. The furniture was made of dark wood. There were paintings on the walls whose landscapes were covered in a film of grey that had grown over years and years, and a picture of a half-dressed woman on a motorbike which also came from another time, and the cups and plates, painted with flowers, were chipped and mazed with cracks like the lines on the back of my eczematous hands. Everything in my house had been used before it arrived, hand-me-downs from maiden aunts and things found in the road. It was spooky to think about how everything in the house had been used before, the invisible lips that had met the cup, eyes that had rested on the paintings, skirts that had brushed the legs of the chairs. In Clare's home the sofa was soft, the armchairs were soft and the cups were entire. Everything belonged to life. The air that streamed through the nose in my house was thickened with dusty age; in Clare's, it was freshened with floral or citrus or pine.

Clare was a part of me in a literal sense—I carried her knowledge, her likes and dislikes, and her mannerisms, often because I deliberately copied her, but also in the form of imitative reflections and responses, which train themselves into any body when it spends a length of time with another, and, lastly, in the sense that I followed her around. By the end of spring even Nic, Clare's mom, was getting tired of us sitting cross-legged, knees touching, on her carpet while we shot down pixelated airplanes. "Why don't you go to your own house?" she teased me. I didn't know how to reply in the same unserious tone. I was ready to play outside and so was Clare, but the days were still short and cold rain came down onto wet ground. Spring was coming, though, not only because the human children were getting bored with *Sonic the Hedgehog*, but also because the cows were out, if briefly, on the day that the younger Gray farmer, Alice's son, knocked on my parents' door and asked with hasty, pressurized civility, could we help him bring the cows back in. They had only just been released into the fields for the warmer part of the year and it seemed that the fences had failed over the winter because several posts were down and the cows were in the wood. The wood was public property but this wouldn't have unduly worried Thomas Gray were it not for the fact that it was wild garlic time. I didn't like the flavor of garlic, but even I could understand the allure of those fat leaves, saturated with cold water. The garlic, said the farmer in this mannered, compressed voice, would flavor the milk for weeks, just at the moment when the spring grass should give it a taste that would be rich and deliciously neutral.

We went out into the wood and I was placed on top of a gate with a hazel stick where the adults would drive the cows through. I thought that I was the ringmaster, high up on my gate, but of course I was being stored where I wouldn't get in the way.

The floor of the wood, spread out to one side, was filled with green waves of wild garlic rising as a sharp peppery scent which told me, in its distinct and intense tone, that things were beginning to grow. Dead-nettles appeared in the brighter light along the fence, in front of the trees. Each one had a collar of white flowers which, when pulled out individually and held close to the eye, were shaped like a brass instrument attached at the mouthpiece to the stalk and right there, where a tiny mouth could meet the back of each tiny white trumpet, was one gold dot of sugary liquid. When I dabbed it on the tip of my enormous tongue I could taste its saccharine point. The wood was preparing itself, plant by plant, day by lengthening day, to be consumed.

Right beside me there was one small island of wood anemones which clung together in a stand against the rippling expanse of garlic. The anemones hung their cupped flowers downward, like bells. They were white with a bluish tint, and to this day I have never since seen so many of them growing so close together, and never in these bluish tones. They had a modest look, bowing their heads to hold their ground against the tongue-shaped garlic leaves that stood tall around them. The flowers were so fragile that it was clear that their strength was in whatever lay underground, holding in intricate rhizomatic affiliations against the looser networks of the larger plants. The anemones were poisonous. As I looked down on them I felt myself swept up in the air and into an airplane flying over a green prairie interrupted by a deep blue lake—it was the wood, and not my mind, which took me through these scales, from the pinprick of nectar to the earth's surface, and gave me the shock of finding myself still on my own two flat feet with the leaves crushing under the weight of my body, the smell of garlic and wet earth rising in a trail behind me when I climbed back onto the gate and stood on the top bar, from which I could see over to the edge of the quarry and down to the water at its base.

The cows ran past swiftly and quietly. When they were back in their field Mr. Gray said that there was nothing more to do. He spoke evenly and thanked us more than once for the help. He kept pressing his lips together and one hand rose repeatedly to smooth one eyebrow into place. We passed through the farmyard on our way home. Beside the barn there was a group of friendly-looking brown hens, hens who sometimes wandered out along the verges and whose bodies made me think of dark, lukewarm teapots. There was only one hen who was not brown and that day she was being attacked. She was slim, with black and white marbled feathers, though it was difficult to see her because she was half hidden by the brown hens that surrounded her. Their beaks vanished into the depths of feathers and then reappeared, bloodied. They were making an unearthly sound: the attackers, as much as the victim, sounded upset. Years later I read Primo Levi's response to a question he was often asked when he gave talks about his experiences in Auschwitz: people wanted to know why it happened, and Levi's thoughtful and complex answer begins with an animal and perhaps insurmountable fear of small differences.

Small differences were becoming more real at school, where the quick children were already being separated from the slow and the girls from the boys. The school computer had divided us again. Ann, who was the best at reading and writing, who knew the answers to many of the teacher's questions, was afraid of the computer. When compelled to use it she sat stiffly on its chair, swiveling fractionally from one side to another and splaying her hands across the whole apparatus, then stabbing the keys with an index finger, like a bird, randomly pecking. She would shake her head, bewildered or angry, when the thing she needed to happen didn't.

Meanwhile John Green, who sat in silence when we were asked to spell aloud the tricky words, or when quizzed on general knowledge, had a different version of intelligence—he boasted about driving a combine, taking a car engine apart and putting it back together, or straightening a foal that was stuck in the birth canal. He knew mechanisms of all kinds, especially those of the animal bodies—he was already explaining sex to the playground. That's why it hadn't taken him long to grasp the logic of the computer's simple commands.

This inversion of intelligence didn't upset us children. We already had different standards of knowledge for the playground, the classroom, the home, or the wood, and different hierarchies in each of these places. For the teachers, who believed knowledge to be general, the situation was unsettling. One day when Ms. Carr's class were outside doing PE, Ms. Carr came into our classroom and politely asked a girl in the year above me, Amy, to remove herself from the computer. Mrs. Hepton glanced up from the teacher's desk and greeted Ms. Carr, who told her that she had a document she needed to type up. She would sit quietly at the computer, it wouldn't take long. Ms. Carr had a large yellowing bruise on her face and we were in the middle of silent exercises in our workbooks, and so many pairs of eyes followed her with interest.

Ms. Carr sat at the computer, called up a document, and typed a few words. Then she halted, half-turned in the chair. I could see that she was examining the keyboard with a baffled look on her face, as though certain letters had gone missing. Eventually, she spoke.

"What's the one for crossing out a word?"

Clare put up her hand.

"The square delete button on the right-hand side," she said.

There was some more typing and then another long pause. I watched Ms. Carr and I could see Clare, in front of me, watching her too. The unbruised side of Ms. Carr's face was red and glazed with light sweat. Individual auburn hairs stuck to the temple. She was not her usual cool, tall, thin, pale self.

"Clare," she said. "Come here, stand here."

Ms. Carr murmured something in Clare's ear and Clare, watching the screen, took the mouse into her small hand.

The document was not long. Ms. Carr soon rose from the chair and instructed Clare to print it. She stood to wait while the printer warmed up, leaving the seat in front of the computer vacant.

Mrs. Hepton told Amy that she could return to the computer to complete her session. Amy, who was sitting in the front row, had the lid of her desk raised, and so she didn't notice Ms. Carr approaching. Ms. Carr flicked down the lid of the desk so that it slammed hard. There was a loud crack and a very short, very high scream. Then the lid was down and Amy was looking at her curled red fingers.

"You can work on the computer," said Ms. Carr, "when you've learned to read and write." Her gaze swept the room. "One half of this class is barely literate."

The bruise on her face darkened to the color of a storm cloud. I looked away, out of the window, at the cherry trees in the playground which were, with great expertise, releasing drifts of browning pink blossom into their surroundings. A cherry tree, I realized, would teach itself to recite multiplication tables, or start fires, or express fear, if it had any good reason to do so.

There were only two children who could use the computer and also read books with ease. Clare was one and the other was Ashley, Ash, the only child in the school who was not white. His parents came from Leicester and his mother's parents were Ugandan Asian. The only sizeable minority communities who were known locally were the Indian and Pakistani communities in the industrial towns to the west. Tensions in these towns, like those of the mining communities, made themselves felt remotely in the surrounding areas, of which my village was an outlying part. There was a sense of apprehension about immigration, as though there were armies gathering on the other side of the horizon. The children were aware of this. It manifested in the playground in the things that were avoided in Ash's presence. Ash did not see himself as South Asian and yet the other children did not address to him the jokes about those communities which went around, and which must have originated with the parents. One day on the school bus Ash had a disagreement with a boy called Lee. I didn't see its cause. What I remember is the moment the bus parked up in our village and Lee, who was at the front of the line, directed at Ash a disjointed list of racialized words as he ran down the steps.

It was rare and shocking because it was open. The rest of us quickly, quietly responded to close it down. We didn't catch one another's eyes as a girl murmured conciliatory things to Ash, a boy shouted something back at Lee. Our collective response was consistent with the recitation *You can't say that* at the end of a racist joke, a recitation which was inevitable but also gleeful because it allowed the conversation to move in both directions at once—to tell the joke while withdrawing it and removing ourselves, personally, from any association with this aggression, while allowing it to snowball, while rolling the snowball together. Meanwhile in school assembly we sang confused songs about how children could be black or white and it didn't make any difference: people all over the world should be treated the same because they were all the same. There were white people who came from different places too, and here any hint of difference—a name, a food, or an accent which expanded the local range—was received with studied indifference. The only thinkable solution to the world's unevenness was to assert that everything, everywhere, was exactly the same.

I don't want to speculate about what this situation was like for Ash or his sister or his parents because I have heard too little about what it is like to live in a place where those who live around you do not look like you, and people who are said to look like you do not understand where you come from. Rural minority populations were small, and they weren't given many services or support, or even the dignity of being recognized as communities, but perhaps living as a part of something too small to be seen was also a form of resistance or a means of escape. I can only describe what manifested in my presence and the thing that I was present with was Ash's family's sense of humor—I can't remember his parents in any mode other than advanced and exquisite sarcasm. His mother Elizabeth worked in the old people's home on the edge of the village and sometimes she permitted Ash and me to come into the small yard at the back of the building where the caregivers parked their cars, while we waited for her to finish. We sat on the step, looking into the laundry room where Elizabeth moved up and down the double-height row of washing machines, drawing steaming sheets out with occasional yelps at the heat of the boil-wash. Gusts of Persil air billowed from the door. She wore a sugar-pink tunic which I thought was the most desirable item of clothing I had ever been lucky enough to witness. She made it so, with her long neck, her cropped hair and the impression she gave of absolute superiority in the situation, which included my gazing eye as she rose above and beyond me, occasionally turning outside not to keep an eye on me or even on her son, but to check in on the activities of goldfinches and yellowhammers on the bird-feeders she had hung from the black metal fire escape. She never asked us to help her.

Her husband Rich worked at a bed-and-breakfast and I believed that he went there every morning, but I only ever saw him outdoors on one occasion. At home, in the afternoons he would sit beside the fire in his white shirt and checkered trousers, his skin so pale that it had a luminous quality, almost blue, and his fine straight black hair lightly greased. As far as I ever saw he passed the expanse of the day mining a pile of the previous day's newspapers, which he had brought home from work, for a selection of choice ironies to share with his wife. Each delivery was honed and planed to deadpan. In that household there was no such thing as direct praise and the most severe criticism imaginable was to hear Elizabeth describe somebody or something as *keen*. She and Rich were the queen and king of this strenuously laid-back humor, though a diluted version of it was apparent in many households. Jobseeking or joblessness were a basic ground and the community, at least in public, imposed on itself the appearance that finding and retaining work was a droll game for adults. Shifts, childcare, job center officers, bosses, and hours were there to be played, beaten, dodged, delayed, or lost. When adults ran into one another in the street or at the school bus stop, I would hear them exchange a recent play or gambit. It was a collective story, more for others than for one's own sake. When Nic, Clare's mother, got a new job, I told my parents at teatime and they both put their cutlery down.

"That's wonderful," my father said.

"Oh, she must be so relieved," said my mother.

I made them guess what it was. My clue was that the job was easy. "I can't believe you even get paid for it. Potato-picking."

My father picked up his fork again and spoke to his food: "That's backbreaking work."

Matthew, who lived next door, worked away on short-term contracts, and when he was at home, waiting for his next job, he put his energy into his garden. He smashed up the concrete garden path that ran from the front door to the gate and then carried the rubble, piece by piece, to the edges of surrounding arable fields, where he dumped it. He dug out a small pond, lined it with garbage bags, and populated it with newts, frogs, and a plastic floating decoy duck. He planted a tiny yew tree and gave my mother clippings from it—rosemary, he said: the movement of its mildly poisonous clippings through our intestines, over the following years, mapped out the physical passage of his frustrated sense of humor. He planted cabbages, raspberry canes, horticultural blackberries, spinach, and potatoes. Soldier, the dog, was respectful of the beds; she never dug them up or even walked across them. He grew a lawn from seed, pegging it out so that he could calculate the correct volume of seed, and then protecting it from pigeons with chicken wire. It was almost a disappointment to me, in adult life, to learn that you can throw the seed on the ground in random handfuls and the grass grows anyway.

One day when this lawn was mature, I came home from school before my parents—they must have both had some temporary post—and there was a girl outside, lying with her head on our side of the grass and her feet on Matthew's. The girl was wearing pale, worn blue jeans, lying on the grass with her head resting on a large backpack and a scarf over her face to keep off the sun. She sat up and drew her knees in to her chest and examined my face.

"Do you know who I am?"

"Teresa," I said.

She shook her head and laughed.

"Serena."

She nodded, pleased: she'd won again.

It was one of their twin things—they would both ask me, when they visited or telephoned: "Do you know who I am?" I don't know whether each knew that the other did it.

Serena and Teresa said that they were my big sisters. We didn't share any blood, but I knew the official terms of the relationship, that they were my father's ex-girlfriend's daughters. He had helped to raise them for a while but he wasn't that much older than them. Sometimes a twin would turn up and stay for a day or a week.

"I've got a present for you," said Serena. "I've carried it on my back, all the way from France. But first, I'm desperate, can you show me where the key's hidden?"

When my parents arrived home we went to the pub. The adults sat in the garden and I went to play with Ann, whose house was on the same road.

When Ann went in for her tea I slipped back through the beer garden gate and joined the adults on the wooden bench. My mother was talking but she finished as I approached.

"Why don't you just move?" Serena asked.

My mother chuckled and looked at my father. My father shrugged. They both looked back at Serena as though she might have something to tell them.

Serena smiled and started to roll a cigarette. "No, I mean it's lovely to be rooted." She turned to me. "I like moving through different places." She started to tell me about the long train journey she was about to go on, through mountains and ice and deserts.

My father, interrupting, asked Serena how she would pay for the trip and she said, "Seasonal work." She licked along the edge of the cigarette paper, then picked threads of tobacco off her tongue. "I've been at a café in Toulouse all spring."

IT WAS DARK WHEN WE got home. I was on my way to bed when Serena called me back. "Your present!"

I could see it, sharp corners poking through the backpack's fabric. She slid it out, it wasn't wrapped. A heavy book. We sat on the floor and turned the pages together: color reproductions of ancient pictures found on the walls of caves and rocks.

Serena turned the pages too fast and I had to hold her wrist so that I could take each image in. They were simple, serious pictures of animals and humans doing things separately and together, mostly stalking one another. Some of the painters made prints from their own bodies. I did not recognize the animals, and said so. One looked like a massive cow who had not been dehorned. Serena explained that most of the mammals in the pictures had been hunted out of existence.

That book is one of the few things I still own from that time. I can see its golden spine on the shelf to my left while I am writing this. It's April and I'm not allowed to leave the house more than once a day, for a short period of physical exercise, but I don't make use of the official allowance: I haven't been outside now for sixteen days. I have been instructed to shelter in place. The sun is hot and I have pulled down the broken blind and jammed it into the window frame so that the light can't get in, but it does. Bright rays pierce the small opening where the jammed blind leaves a space and it projects an image on the blank back wall of the room. Because it is dark inside the room and bright outdoors the image on the back wall is hyperdistinct. It wavers very slightly, supernaturally, but I've spent a long time staring out at the view, so I know the forms that are painted on the back wall even with my back turned to them, the small walled yards, the alleyway with the trash stores belonging to the low-rise apartment block on the road that is parallel to mine.

At night they are all illuminated and I see them more clearly than I do during the day. There are young parents with toddlers and tropical fish and in another apartment an older couple—a man who looks, from this distance, very much like Jürgen Klopp, who this morning moved his tomato seedlings from the inside to the outside windowsill, and the woman he lives with who, from here, bears a slight resemblance to Indira Gandhi—she spends hours at her sewing machine at the window. In the top-floor apartment there is a woman who lives alone, like me. Above her roof I can see the upper bodies of the lime trees behind her building—their greyish images are also wavering on my back wall now. Within the trees I see crows, magpies, pigeons, and squirrels flowing along the lateral branches. Obscured behind all that there is the inner beltway that surrounds the city and is quieter than usual now. Nonetheless traffic sounds reach me in here. If a car was to drive along that road and stay on it as it turned on to the freeway, in thirty minutes or so this car would reach the place where I used to live, which I have been describing here. No cars will go there right now, since only urgent travel is permitted, and so space no longer feels regular or continuous—it's broken. This area I look out on is divided into bordered zones. Laws hold us all in place and forbid us from going to another. Our separation means little to the virus in the atmosphere, a virus so tiny that it is impossible to see it on my lips and so huge that it is impossible to see it crossing continents. Scientists on the news say that it evolved inside a pangolin's body, from a reservoir in a *Rhinolophus* bat. The novel virus, a chimera, crossed another species boundary at the end of last year, when it began to communicate itself through human bodies. Now it's here, in my surroundings, and we are all living inside that pangolin, everybody in my neighborhood: pigeons, Klopp, squirrels, tomato plants, sound waves, books, bookshelves, sewing machine, blue waterweeds, and the lone woman on the top floor. I've never noticed that I am sharing this space with so many others before and I wish I could be out there among them now. But the authorities say that the world is fatally interconnected and inside, alone with my thoughts, is the safest place to be. In some ways the world feels more alive and vivid to me now than when I was out there, in it with all the other people, animals, birds, plants, insects, and machines.

In the morning Serena and I left the house together: I had to catch the school bus and she had a flight booked. We parted at the bottom of the drive, she kissed the top of my head, and then I walked on, glancing once over my shoulder to see her framed on either side with brown wallflowers, roses the color of new blood, and the flowers that Matthew called red-hot pokers, which he had planted during his periods out of work. Around the lawn, behind his flowerbeds, he had planted a few thin young trees: cherry, mountain ash, and one silver birch. He had built a redbrick patio and trained a clematis up the side of his house; it grew across to ours, trailing below my parents' bedroom window. He had taken down the garage that had been at the top of the drive and disposed of the asbestos sheets behind the lilac trees, which he pruned with a chainsaw. Every morning he went running with Soldier around the track that looped the wood—in theory. In reality the track only went so far, there was a point at which it became boggy and impassable, where the Forestry Commission trucks had to park up and people had to turn back and retrace their footsteps.

Early this year, just a few weeks before the lockdown began, I was talking to a doctor who worked at an end-of-life hospice and he talked to me about how family members respond to grief. He said that some enter into their loss, reflect on it, and spend time grieving, but others "keep busy"—the doctor put it in scare quotes with his fingers—by exercising, joining clubs, working long hours, and gardening. I wonder how many gardens are being dug over, pets adopted from shelters, pets returned to shelters, plants pruned, seedlings nurtured or overwatered, trees planted and logs chopped, as a living manifestation of grief, though of course Matthew wasn't mourning any human body. It was the ghost of his other life which was reflected in his pond, buried in his vegetable plot, commemorated in the compost heap that he built out of packing pallets at the back of the house and which he turned once with my help. At least he made something beautiful out of this absence, and it was only when I was older and tried and failed to reproduce parts of Matthew's creation in a rented allotment that I realized he had a gift. I'd lived with it for years without seeing it. All the plants grew for him, he created conditions in which they wanted to. Inside the compost there lived tiny beings and he told me about them—smaller than the eye could see. *As-per-gill-o-sis*. "They're mostly good for the earth and plants and people, but sometimes, if a human body is weak, they can take it over from the inside and then you'd die."

I didn't think much of that. Perhaps there are people who enjoy being given information they have not requested. If so, I have not met these people. I was interested in the things that I could see, the things I already knew about. Once we put too much wet matter into the compost and the tiny beings couldn't or wouldn't do their work. Matthew dug out the sloppy mess and remade it with shredded brown paper. The garden had its own language in which to feed instructions back.

When the compost heap was full it became a platform. From my backyard I could climb up onto it, and from there drop over the fence into the scrubby field behind our houses. Whoever owned the field seemed to have no interest in it, though it can't have been left like that long because no trees had grown, only tall grasses which died back to straw in winter and in spring came up green, yellow, and purple with waving seed-heads, with rosebay willow herb growing high over my head and releasing fluff that drifted out of the back field and into the surrounding village and woods. The field wasn't used by people because the ground was tussocky, with high wet grasses. Even the commuters who walked their dogs didn't go into it. So it was a free run for wild animals and children. Down at the base of the grasses there were smoothed tunnels where the stalks formed themselves around squat furry bodies. These tunnels weren't visible from above. Crawling through the grass, I could look along them but I was the wrong size to use them as passages and the animals didn't pass through in the daytime. I once found a mess of grasses in a clearing and a disembodied grey wing, no blood, the only evidence of a fatal nocturnal drama.

When I came out of the field and climbed back over the pallets into my garden I had grains and teasels sticking to my clothes and in my tangly hair, sometimes inside my mouth. The weeds scraped themselves on any moving body, I can't have been the only animal whose hair was densely seeded with fluff and grasses by plants who took advantage of the opportunity to make their own passages. The seeds dropped away easily once they had emerged from the field. Many would be buried deep in the walls of a burrow, far away from daylight, others fell onto the concrete of the yard when I flicked them off carelessly, others went into the trash via the threads of hair on the back of the hairbrush paddle. Only one or two might have a life story to tell, coming away from a fox's body to grow on a quiet patch of earth at the edge of the wood, or, from my hair, find its way to a landfill, falling out of a split bag to sprout.

One day the elder trees which grew along the back fences around the edge of the field were cut back. The new hedge had a brutal appearance because the elder was brittle and broke with sharp, splintered edges, like snapped bones. A tall sign was erected on the road side of the field. On the front of it there was an artist's impression, in watercolor, of a row of new houses. This sign was equal in size and shape to another sign which was put up at the head of the quarry, which bore no image, only a plain red and white logo. The signs seemed to have some relationship with one another.

The old machines in the quarry, a blue digger and a red dump truck, were driven up from the floor and parked in a niche in the track leading to the road, where they sat like toys on a shelf. They were old, the paint gone patchy with rust. The tipper used to trail black smoke each time it took a load through the village and the digger screamed whenever its arm was engaged. Parked on the track, they kept quiet and stayed still, and days passed. Eventually I realized that they were never again going to work in the quarry, for as long as I lived there, but they kept on changing.

One morning in late winter, I was on the school bus passing the top of the quarry when I noticed, out of the corner of my eye, a difference in this landscape which turned my head. The digger was an emaciated version of the self it had been the day before: somebody must have been in the night and stripped the sheet metal for scrap. The dump truck's bodywork was perhaps made of some less valued material because it remained untouched, standing beside the skeleton of its partner, degrading at a pace too slow for me to see it happening. After school Clare and I would sometimes sit on the fence facing the vehicles, not talking, working our way through handfuls of stones that we aimed, one by one, at the windscreens. We took it in turns, taking time to listen to the skittering sound, or the occasional crack, and, very rarely, to admire a new small hole that had been punched in the glass. Beside us stood the plain logo sign. Nothing else changed on the ground around it.

The housing development in the back field evolved more quickly. Within a year the image of houses on the sign was translated into a row of real houses, the buildings rising and changing the face of the landscape over the course of a few weeks in springtime, as the weeds had grown from nothing to meters tall the spring before.

It was Clare's father, Dmitri, who told me that the two pieces of land—the field and the quarry—had the same owner, and had been sold off at the same time, the field to a housing developer, the quarry to a Canadian engineering company. I had not noticed that the land around the quarry had similar terrain to the back field (scrubby weeds and brown grasses) or that they were almost continuous with one another. Dmitri said that the Canadians had expensive equipment which would stem the leak by lining the problem part with a waterproof barrier. Then they could begin to quarry again on the other side. Dmitri had a beer in his hand that day. It was the only time I ever saw him drink. I caught his feeling of optimism, the springtime feeling of a future opening out for the place, shadowed by an intimation, also, that patients revive in the days before death. When the Canadians closed the quarry for a month to drain it Dmitri, along with the other workers, was suspended on full pay. During this period a delegation from the Canadian company visited the quarry. I was at school that day and was disappointed to hear that the Canadians were not real Canadians but English representatives of the company, which had operations in every continent. They renamed the quarry after their company. The company's sites were family members, with relatives of the same name living in North America, Europe, and Africa. The quarry had never had a name before. Clare's dad said that they could call it what they liked.

When I got home I saw the changes. At one side of the quarry there was a concrete mixer and bags of powder, and there was a huge plastic curtain, half rolled up, similar to that with which Matthew's garden pond was lined, but on a different scale. Above them the dump truck was perceptibly changing on its own timetable. The rust had crept out and the paint retreated, the tires had gently lowered toward the ground. In summer, single-stalk plants grew in the back. The following spring a thrush nested in the hollow of the cracked black leather seat. It was a good nest—wide and messy, with drips of white shit all over the seat. The thrush flew in and out through a small, round hole in the windscreen which was ideally sized, as though it had been created just for her, because it was too small for a predator. When she exited she flew right over the fence on which Clare and I used to sit. We must have been like furniture there because Mr. Gray came out one day to find us. He stopped at a distance up the road, whistled, and beckoned us over.

Clare and I followed him back to the haystack in his yard. There, inside a nest, kittens rolled around their mother, grey, orange, and brown. Mr. Gray leaned in and grabbed two. They hung vulnerably from his finger and thumb, separate and very small. One striped, one tortoiseshell, with a strange, pointy face and tiny ears. Mr. Gray handed the stripy one to me. Its compact, squirming body felt more fish than mammal and I quickly returned it to its mother and waited for Clare, but her head was bent over the tortoiseshell and she was whispering something fierce and secret. The mother cat, spread out in a loose C-shape to allow the remaining kittens to feed, looked relaxed. She tipped her head back and kept half-open eyes on us but she didn't move or protest. "Ten pounds each," said Mr. Gray.

MY MOTHER SAID YES. I stood blindsided for a moment, my fists relaxing at my sides. She turned back to her work. "The kitten should stay with its mother until it's finished drinking milk," she said.

I told her that Mr. Gray had told me that the cats were ready to go now. "We can give it cream."

My mother looked up again.

"He says they have to go now," I said.

There was a moment's hesitation or calculation, and then my mother agreed, in a tone of voice that told me she believed it was not right. She found the money and then I went back out to call on Clare.

From the road I could see Nic, sitting in her usual place on the front step, and Clare, with her back to me, kneeling in front of her mother, thin dress in the dust, bawling. Nic looked exasperated. "I'm sorry," she said. "Not after the hamsters."

I halted at the garden gate. Nic noticed me and rolled her eyes, as though we were equals and both victims of Clare's outrageous expectations. I took this as permission to approach and perched myself on the step beside Nic. Clare continued to cry noisily for a period and then, without being prompted or comforted, she stopped and wiped her face with the dusty hem of her dress, turning to show me her profile.

"I'll help you choose yours," she said in an emptied voice. She went inside to use the toilet and then came back out, still wearing her grave expression and still not allowing my eyes to see hers.

The cats were in the same place but Mr. Gray had disappeared. We walked around the farm, calling. By the side of his van there was a group of hens and they were fighting again, just as they had been the last time I was there. I tried to locate the marbled hen at the center but I couldn't. Then I realized that she was in the circle, viciously pecking a victim I couldn't see.

Mr. Gray came around the corner and kicked his boot toward the hens, who scattered. He picked up the victim. It was a brown hen, like the others.

"They always bully the new ones for a while," Mr. Gray said to me.

The bullies surrounded him, fluttering in spurts, ruffling their feathers and chattering. The marbled hen was one of them. I looked at them all. I could see no logic to it. Perhaps there was no logic at all. Perhaps I was only thinking about hens.

Then Clare's voice came from beside the haystack.

"I will have the tortoiseshell," she said.

She was standing upright and waving a ten-pound note. She held her gaze, steadily, on Mr. Gray.

Automatically my hand went to my pocket, half expecting that my own money would be gone, but it was there. I extended it toward Mr. Gray.

"I want the stripy one," I said.

"Do your mothers say you can?" As he spoke he took the money from our hands.

Clare and I exhaled a unified *Yes*.

Mr. Gray looked at me for a moment, then looked at Clare. He drew breath, as though he was about to say something, but then he half-turned away with a shrugging motion and pushed the money into his back pocket.

"Thank you, ladies," he said. "Which ones did you say you wanted?"

We left the farm in the pink of early evening. On the construction site the builders had gone home. Cradling our kittens in cupped hands, Clare and I went inside the shell of one of the half-built houses where we couldn't be seen. Within the walls (no roof yet) there was a small pallet of slabs of local Yorkstone. I recognized it and knew that it came from up on the industrial moors out west and was used on the facing of the houses that were close to completion. The pack was open and accessible to anybody who came in through the open doorway. Opposite, taking up most of the interior room, there was a much larger cube of blocks of a different stone. It was almost identical to the Yorkstone, though cut into smaller, thicker rectangles. The large cube was wrapped in clear plastic, secured with bands on which were printed some characters I couldn't interpret and, in English, *Qingdao Chevin sandstone "Yorkstone"*.

Clare and I sat down on the concrete floor between the two monuments. The floor was new, its rough surface prickled my bare legs, and I examined the tiny cushions on the bottom of my kitten's foot.

"It's a paw print," I said, surprised, and Clare said "Duh."

We allowed the tiny cats to explore the house. I asked Clare where she'd taken the money from and she glared at me. I asked her what she was going to do and she said, "What are *we* going to do?" Her kitten returned to her, mewing, and butted her knee. She—Clare had decreed that it was a girl—climbed inside Clare's crossed legs, which made a hollow the size of a small cat-basket. Clare looked up at me, gleaming with triumph, and a cat-sized space, hollow, dry, and safe, opened up inside my mind.

"I know where you can keep her," I said.

I ADORED MY OWN KITTEN and so did my parents. He took possession of our home, threw objects off the shelves, and felled some raspberry canes. I loved him but I did not identify with him as I did with Clare's kitten, whose existence was more honest than that of my own kitten. He lorded it around a house which wasn't exactly his. Meanwhile Clare's kitten lived in secret inside our tree. We placed a stolen roof tile across the entrance to the hollow. Clare fed her on cat food from the village shop, I don't know where she found the money for it. We visited together every day and I helped Clare to feed the kitten, to pick out the dirt from the hollow with a folded leaf as best we could, to return the kitten and slot the tile back in place. This all went on for some indeterminate period of time—the time we spent there was not drawn into the calendars or timetables of home and school lives. I knew how it would turn out and I believe Clare did too. It was Clare, after all, who had told me to put the baby rabbit back when I removed it from its mother. But we also knew what had happened to the kittens we hadn't chosen. Children understand most things but can't articulate much. Clare and I were developing the ability to express ourselves and our ability to listen was in decline. There was no wild place or natural habitat to which the little cat could return. The relevant fact was this: I was allowed a kitten and Clare wasn't. I had no grounds on which to tell her what to do.

The back door of my house was made of panes of frosted glass, revealing a warped version of the outside. It was a warm evening, between spring and summer, when a dark and pale blur, unmistakably Clare, appeared on the other side, startling me as I went from the kitchen to the toilet. Clare rarely called on me—it was usually the other way round.

She hadn't knocked and so she must have been waiting. When I opened the door she spoke in a rasping whisper: "She's escaped. Now a fox will get her."

She started to cry—not sobbing, as she had when her mother said she couldn't have a cat—but quietly streaming tears as though her body was draining itself. It's the only time I've seen tears like that. They didn't fall in drops but flowed constantly, a single body of water running from each eye, and when I looked at it, it became all that I could see; it did, actually, look like a river, and I wouldn't have been surprised to notice a tiny flash of blue and orange flitting across, or to see an infinitesimal silver fin rise up to break the surface. I don't remember comforting her. I think I just stood there with her while she cried, looking over her shoulder at the mud mountain in the back field.

The mudheap had grown tall as the housing development developed. It became the size of two houses, beautiful, a mountain to the quarry's valley, and the builders didn't remove it even as the houses gained wiring, doors, and windows. That spring and summer, when Clare kept and then lost her kitten, she and I slid down that mudheap, getting faster and bolder until the day I flipped over the edge and landed on my back. When I stood up my neck hurt and there was a ringing in my ears.

Clare was still at the top of the heap.

"Let's go to mine," she said.

I shook my head. I wanted to go home.

Clare descended and came close to inspect me.

"Listen," she said in a low voice. "There's something wrong with your house."

"I swallowed the Juicy Fruit," I said.

Clare looked quickly into my eyes and her face was scared. We both knew that swallowing chewing gum would kill you.

"Will you come?"

She shook her head.

I ran back to the garden fence. From the top of Matthew's compost heap I turned back to look. Clare was still standing and staring at me, her arm across her body protectively, one hand holding the opposite elbow.

"There's something wrong with your house," she said again. I nodded, which made the metallic line of sound inside my head rise and fall. After the summer holidays Clare was due to go up into Ms. Carr's class and would not be able to be seen with me at school anymore.

When I looked down at my feet in the compost, I could see puffs of steam or spores around them. I could feel the tiny beings that Matthew had warned me about, the beings which took advantage of a weakened body to attack. They swarmed around me, into my lungs, right through the bones in my hurt arm, and into my stomach, where the chewing gum lurked and radiated its fatal particles.

I ran inside. Unable to find anybody and frantic, I called out about the compost heap and the chewing gum.

My father put his head around the door.

"You don't need to worry about the germs," he said. "You'll probably pass the chewing gum, if it was only one piece." He was smiling.

WHEN THE MUDHEAP DISAPPEARED, THE new homes were finished and people moved in. The homes had shared front gardens and so it was inevitable that hedges went up to divide one from another with cruel equality. Ruler-straight rows of trees which looked like small, literally pointless Christmas trees were cute at first, standing waist-high so that neighbors could talk over them, but they weren't Christmas trees, they were leylandii and they shot up at the pace of a machine. Soon the neighbors could not see one another and many houses were in the shade of dark green and yellow walls that enlarged the space between them, which had not, previously, been a space at all. The hedges were cut at sharp angles, creating neat living geometries across whose flat surfaces small spiders spun their webs. Nobody plants leylandii out of love for their form or flourishing, they're living expressions of passive aggression: live walls. They've done well for themselves out of human enmity, like all those other natural forms that proliferate with human misery, *bacillus anthracis*, ricin, prussic acid, or gamma rays. Some species, certain fungi and viruses, like rare individual humans, make a life that is so rampantly aggressive that it can be difficult to see such a lifeway as the strenuous effort to survive in a merciless environment, easier to call it an expression of character. Between the new houses, the flourishing leylandii sucked the life from the soil below them and blocked out the light with their dense thick boughs. They were too internally cramped and dusty to support playing children or offer the birds a place in which to hide. They didn't produce flowers, fruit, or nuts. The wood grew very quickly, which was convenient when founding a hedge, but there was a flaw in its rapid progress.

One winter I saw a branch break off after heavy snowfall and drop onto a car, denting the hood and leaving a broken branch which exposed its light, brittle wood. I profited off the pride that was embodied in the new cars that stood outside the new houses: I made my first earnings car-washing on the weekends. I enjoyed it because the car owners had clean buckets, sponges, and those blade-like wipers that cause soapy water to fall in a straight line of splatters on the floor. While I washed I watched the inhabitants of the houses and I felt a strong if unjustified sense of superiority over them because I knew the past lives of the place on which their homes stood. I could see, sometimes so clearly that it disturbed me, translucent stems of long grass waving inside the living rooms, willow herb skewering television cabinets, a bedroom buried inside the vanished mudheap like a mouth full of earth.

"Can plants have ghosts?" I asked Alice. Her farm, once in open fields beyond the edge of the village, was now surrounded on two sides by the new estate. Inside her kitchen (brick floor, open fire, black range) nothing felt different.

Alice looked at me as though she did not understand the question. I strained to explain myself. "Like how there are no birch trees in Birch Wood," I said.

"There were never any birch trees in Birch Wood," said Alice.

"Well, there was one."

"But before that, when it was a birch wood."

Alice made a noise in the back of her throat. "No," she said. "The wood was named after one birch tree—not because it was full of birches but because there was only one of them. It faced the village so you could see it. The birch tree stood out because it was silver and there was only one of it."

She came over to me—step, drag—and handed me a plate with a biscuit on it.

"Plants can't be ghosts and neither can people."

As I ate the biscuit I traced the patterns on the plate. Brown, navy, and cream. When I'd finished I turned the plate upside down and looked at the words on the underside. I swallowed.

"Made in China," I read aloud.

WHEN CLARE WENT UP INTO Ms. Carr's class, she and I stopped spending time together. I started to spend more time with larger groups of children. In summer we sometimes took our swimming things to school in the morning in carrier bags and then, in the late afternoon, we would swim or jump off the bridge. It was difficult to get into the river because there was a no-man's-land of mud, bulrushes, and, occasionally, leeches, which I had to make my way through to get to water which was deep enough for swimming. The ankle-deep water was tepid by that time of day and there was something disgusting about the softness of the mud, which had been processed so finely by the river that my foot could hardly feel it. It was like walking through a dark cloud, present to the sense of sight but not to the sense of touch, and this in itself felt horrible, as though the absence of texture was my body's problem rather than a property of the mud. The silky mud supported bulrushes whose reeds were sandpapery—painless, as they pulled themselves along the soft skin of a shin or calf, but when I looked down, I'd see a needle-fine graze that slowly grew heavy with pain. If the mud was disgusting and the rushes could scrape me, it was the leeches that would make me hesitate before stepping in. The leeches were such a dark shade of brown that they were almost black, like dead wood, and on hot days they danced like snakes in a snake charmer's basket, making a ring with the bottom of their bodies, which were small enough to sit on the surface of that light mud. Their upper bodies rose toward the sunlight and wriggled constantly, trees in the wind. In fact, on sunlit days, when the leeches were out, this warm shallow area looked like a miniature enchanted forest, the mud yellow, with green rushes and black swaying leeches wiggling, and cables of sunlight wobbling through them. It *felt* like an enchanted forest, too, in the sense that it took nerve to cross it. Few girls dared to pass the shallows on the days the leeches were out. I tried it one overcast afternoon, when I couldn't see any as I set out, and it was only as my giant foot made contact with the mud, a nuclear cloud of sandy brown spreading through the water from my previous footprint, that I noticed the leech in my way and understood in a heartbeat that I wouldn't miss it. But then, as my foot went down, the leech actually shrank away from me and wrapped itself in a circle around the base of a rush. It faced inward, refusing to be an obstacle on my straight path. I waited, but the leech remained wrapped around the base of the reed, neat as a wedding ring. It wasn't interested in my blood. My feet were gradually sinking into the mud, which was chilled below the surface, and grew colder with every deepening millimeter. Discomfort dawned on me and I noticed that it was only when my foot was in pain that my head was aware of its presence.

My parents would collect me at the river, or they did when their car was starting. There was a telephone box by the side of the road from which I could call the operator to reverse the charges home. My parents occasionally reminded me to take a coin in my bag because reversing charges cost more than double the rate of a normal call, but the calls were always short and my parents always agreed to come. Then one day the telephone rang until it had almost rung itself out, and on the very last ring I heard my mother's voice: "Yes?"

She sounded distracted. I could hear her but I wouldn't be able to speak until the operator put me through.

The operator asked my mother whether she would receive a call from me. My mother asked the operator to repeat herself and the operator reiterated the request. Then there was a pause.

"No," said my mother. "I don't accept the call."

She put the phone down. The line clicked and the operator came back through to me. "The caller doesn't accept the call."

I said nothing.

"Um," said the operator, in a different tone of voice. "How old are you exactly, will you be alright?"

I put the phone down and stood inside the phone box for a moment, watching the receiver rest in its cradle. Black Bakelite, clouded with fingerprints.

During the long walk back I ran through these events in my mind. When eventually I arrived home the sun had set. My mother ran out of the house to meet me. She hugged me and apologized. "We've just had an expensive bill," she said. "I had a pan on."

She hugged me again and then stood back so that she could see my face. I wasn't angry so much as unsettled, as though the river had gained the ability to speak English and told me to get my feet out of its mud.

In colder weather I would stay on the school bus up the hill, passing the edge of the wood at a sharp corner where there was a small, steep field tucked away behind the road. This was the mushroom field, where I went with my father in the late summer, early morning, before school. He looked for the edible mushrooms with feathery tops and brown undersides which were almost identical to the mushrooms that could send you to the hospital or, if eaten in large quantities, kill you. I looked for the red and white mushrooms which were poisonous, which I had seen in picture books and never in real life. I wouldn't see them, he told me, because they only grew in the shadows of pine or birch trees, not here in the open. They liked to live with particular tree roots, he explained. There were invisibly tiny members of the mushroom family on the roots of all the trees—every plant that was alive was sustained by these miniature members of the mushroom family.

I chose to ignore this unrequested information and continued to look for the red mushrooms in the open field and to consider the consumption of mushrooms an evil. I did not like to find mushrooms, though I enjoyed looking for them. They were good at hiding. They flourished at the base of the long grasses, in the shady damp conditions that were anathema to life as I knew it. Those mornings were pearly and golden, with beams of light and trails of mist slipping through one another and between each blade of grass. The slopes were at their peak of greenness, just before they dulled with shorter days and colder weather. I found it difficult to suspend my disbelief when my dad told me that the structures of the mushrooms extended in all directions underground and I tried my best to imagine it, uniform and all-encompassing, like a net, below my feet, wherever I happened to be standing, but I couldn't imagine it because the way the fruiting bodies were distributed seemed so irregular to me. I parted waves of grass in long trails, my jeans getting sodden, until suddenly I'd be surprised by a moon bulging, silky to touch, sometimes alone, sometimes in a perfect circle, which had chosen that particular place for reasons I couldn't work out. Below my feet the underground network of mushroom filaments were growing out from its many tips which were splitting, branching, bypassing, doubling back, or fusing together, as though each tip had its own ideas, though each originated from a single spore. All this seemed mysterious to me—I was a single-minded organism.

We rarely saw other people out on those mornings, but one day I became aware of a presence in the periphery of my vision. When I turned around there were two tall men, one wearing a pale denim jacket, the other carrying a blue-and-white-striped plastic bag. My father turned too and nodded at the men without smiling. They nodded back and we all waded around the field as though unconscious of one another's presence, staring somewhere just beyond our own feet, along the eyeline of the third eye. Then one of the men made a sound and motioned to the rest of us. He'd found a large patch. We gathered together until the patch was almost stripped and then we separated again. The men, my father included, seemed to be content with the silence and it did not feel tense or threatening to me. At no point did they speak or even smile at one another, and the two men left before we did without saying goodbye. I was a girl and therefore I spent more time with women, and so this new experience gave me something to think about. Among the women, silence wasn't empty, it was expressive: it communicated suspicion. If you found yourself in the presence of a woman you didn't know, breaking silence was a necessary act of disarmament. As we walked home my father explained that the men worked on the flower farm and that they had recently arrived from Bulgaria, so perhaps I was wrong—perhaps it was a language barrier.

The flower farm was visible on the other side of the wood. In spring the rows of daffodils sprang out of the heavy clay. From late summer and on into autumn, where I stood to shade my eyes and look across the other side of the valley from the mushroom field, I saw the same fields were full of sunflowers, their petals curling and browning, their centers turning black. The daffodils were bunched up while still frigidly in bud, to be sold at the supermarket, but the sunflowers faded on their stems until the seeds were ripe for birdseed or oil. There was a huge transparent building near the farmhouse: glass, later replaced by plastic sheeting, where the seedlings were raised.

The men who came to work the flower harvest lived in a corner of the flat field, tucked between the plantation edge of the wood and a road into the village. They lived here in spring and again in late summer. It was no place to settle. There were three caravans which the farmer didn't keep well, some wheel arches propped with cinder blocks and the windows covered with a milky plastic that had cracked in places. The people who lived here never appeared in the supposedly public spaces, not the shop or the pub, I never even passed them in the street.

I was thinking about the residents of the flower farm the day we went into lockdown because there were two men working on the building opposite mine. The block of flats is bigger and more solid than the caravans were, so it wasn't the residence itself which reminded me, or the men, who were dressed in hard hats and neon-yellow vests branded with the logo of a public sector services company. It was the wiring: on the side of the building opposite me there was a bundle of wires and I saw their literal connection, via miles of poles, pylons, and lengths of cable, to the single mark of inhabitation that the workers, years earlier, had left on their temporary homes. Somebody clever had strung lines between the caravans, sagging and slung over one another to make a loose asterisk that linked them all. From there, bunched together, the wires had been attached to the telegraph line which ran along the road. A phone line, or some form of energy.

The wiring on the side of the building opposite me is almost identical to what I saw there—most of the wires are clipped to the side of the building, but there is one place at the corner where a fat bunch of soft leads are bundled together with packing tape. The men in the neon vests had been working on it on the day we went into lockdown. They left their cherry-picker parked on the communal grass when they went home that afternoon and of course they didn't come back the following day. The nexus of wires and the cherry picker are still there. I guess they left the job half finished. It looks dangerous to me but I'm not an electrician.

Up above the flower farm on the hill there were wheat fields. I could see these fields from my house, making their way through the months from green to gold. Then, for a single day which felt longer than the entire season, the combine harvester went out. It stayed out through the long evening until the machine had to light up like a boat at sea with its small lights raking the dark massing shadows under a large, dim, pale brown moon. The moon seemed to come alive at that time of year, hanging low in the sky with all its scars in focus, and it was a sphere, not a circle—to see it was to witness a force with a different and uncomfortably familiar agency, like watching a letter *o* float free from its word and bounce across its page with its own volition. Soldier, the dog next door, was dying. She no longer went on her daily runs. Night after night she sat at the side of her kennel, looking upward and making a long, devastated sound. She seemed to be addressing the moon. I was also spooked by it, it was too close and complete.

For one week, tightly bound geometric bales stood on the field where the waves of wheat had been. The bales were alien, straight-edged, casting long shadows in the late summer sun, a statement in which the landscape was not the subject, or even the medium, but the audience. Then one day the first row of bales disappeared. The next day the central row was gone. On the third day, when I got up and looked out of the window, I knew with a sinking feeling that the last would be taken away. What was left was stubble; and although from a distance this looked shiny, almost reflective, I still winced to think about it. Up close, each stumped stalk was thick as a plastic drinking straw and cut at an angle, so that walking bare-legged through it could draw blood. In early autumn most farmers set their stubble on fire and that wheat field on the hill above the flower farm was being burned that day, when I was mushrooming. I liked to see the fields on fire, sometimes half a mile at a time. It had a clean feeling. I had been told—it was generally accepted—that burning the stubble purified the earth for next year's crop. It burned off slugs, germs, molds, and spores. The charred earth and ash that were left behind had the appearance, on a wet autumn day, of a chocolate cake that has been taken out of the oven too soon. Too much and too rich. That year, without preamble, burning the stubble was made a crime.

I knew that it was the last fire. Somebody, scientists or politicians—whoever it was, they were a long way away—had agreed that the smoke polluted the air and the ground and killed off life in the soil, which, they informed us, we all depended on. It was strange or wrong, then, that I felt a sense of release when I watched the stubble burning while I stood in the sloped field with my sole almost touching the mushroom's strange body. Stubble, bale, flame, bedding for farm animals, and bread were all still wheat. I watched the fire eat land that had been quick to harvest, and quicker to burn, and that whole process was part of an annual cycle which rippled on the landscape, which was part of larger geological cycles and radiations that I didn't understand very well. I felt different time frames at work around me, unzipping worlds in different speeds with weird forms of motion, in the way that a train, a butterfly, a mole, a plant, a germ, an explosive, a fire, a child, a fume, discovered space in very different ways. It occurred to me that Monday, Tuesday, and Wednesday, centimeters and meters, were almost random and I was released from gravity, an astronaut clutching my measuring implements as I floated in deep space. There were many moments and no chronology, many places and no orientation. But all this only felt pressing because something in the back of my mind was weighing on me and I went to tug on my dad's hand. It was time to go to school. "I'll miss the bus."

I remained in the lower class and Clare went up to Ms. Carr's, though Ms. Carr had gone away because she was expecting a baby. This was a surprise—she seemed so old. Her face was lined, her hair greying. Too ancient, surely, to be pregnant. But her belly grew big, and she went on leave. A substitute teacher came. That term in Mrs. Hepton's classroom we studied pictures of mushroom clouds. She told us about Hiroshima, radiation therapy, Chernobyl, radon, clean energy, and Nagasaki, all in one week, and explained how the same elements could kill and could give life. Marie Curie, in discovering the cure, gave herself the sickness. Some of this had already entered my consciousness in the form of jokes about the end of the world, Gorbachev's birthmark, deformed babies. Mrs. Hepton held up pictures of clouds advancing from huge continents to our tiny island, and photographs of forests corroded to bony stumps. She told us that the spillage at Chernobyl was first discovered beyond the Iron Curtain not via humans from Kiev or Minsk, but via machines from the south of Sweden, over a thousand miles from the blast. As employees filed into work at a Swedish nuclear power plant, the radiation sensors that scanned their clothing went into overdrive. The workers were puzzled. They tested the radiation detection systems in the different areas of their factory, but nothing seemed to be wrong. They tested their clothing again. Again the alarm bells rang. Their boots were highly irradiated—more so than the other parts of their outfits.

It took time to carry out diagnostic tests, to pin down the precise type of radiation. There were irradiated particles in the grass surrounding the Swedish nuclear power plant, which the employees had walked through on their way to work. Dewdrops brushed onto their boots. The irradiated particles were identified as materials that were used only in the Soviet power plants. Overnight, this radiation had strolled across the globe.

Mrs. Hepton paused, after telling her version of this story, and then explained that acid rain, like radiation, drifted. It was hanging here—she looked up to the ceiling—above our county. It was in the nature of these phenomena to warp or thwart all the living beings that were planted or nurtured in the local area: pregnancies, sugarbeet, potatoes, pine trees. Naturally, all problems were foreign, even if they happened at home, and so it was inevitable that we tried to solve problems on the other side of the world.

Mrs. Hepton acquired a row of potted plants which she placed on the low cabinet at the side of her classroom. She used a glass bottle of liquid feed, silver scissors, and a small copper watering can to tend the plants while the class worked in silence. I grew used to their presence, and then one day she instructed the class to look at them. She explained that the plants grow in the Amazon rainforest, and she named them. A rubber tree, a banana, aralia. The umbrella tree and the spider plant. "Today we will all make posters to Save the Rainforest."

I copied the plants nearest to my desk. The leaves were oval and thick and they lolled. I noticed a film of dust on them. The plants stood peacefully on the cabinet. They did not need to compete with one another or with any neighbors, human, nonhuman, mechanical. None of the things that we drew on our posters, copied from pictures cut out of magazines. No insects or spiders or snakes, no big cats, no pools of opaque green water, no papery leaves fallen between the trees, no mossy rocks, no dripping ferns, no rubber-taps, no long rope-like plants connecting one to another, nothing being harvested from them. At the beginning of the summer holidays we moved them one by one to stand outside, on the concrete, as nobody would be in school to water them.

Along the crest of the mushroom hill there was a low hedge with holly trees growing out of it at intervals along the line of an old path that cut over the top of the hill where the road had to curve the long way around it. Somebody had told me that the hollies, standing tall and evergreen above the hedge, had been planted centuries earlier to mark out the path for walkers when winters were worse than they are now. In those days, for weeks at a time, deep snow hid the paths and hedges so that all directions looked the same. Whoever had planted these trees had situated them with care: as you reached one, the next was in clear view, though the line wasn't necessarily visible all at once. I wondered whether the trees knew of one another—if there was a way that some species of message could be relayed, using the mushrooms' underground network of roots like a telephone line. It seemed possible that there was, though less possible that the trees had any sense of what it was to be a holly among hollies in the way I saw them, which was mostly as those defensive leaves, growing close together over the lower, whiplike green or silver branches, then dispersing near the top of the tree where sheep and deer can't reach and so the leaves have smoother edges. The size of the trees declined as they rose up the hill because the higher ones were stunted by the weather. If the holly trees did communicate, it is unlikely that they had a sense of how the line of them, taken as a collective whole, became a path. Even to humans, that meaning had atrophied by the time I was born, when nobody needed to cut across the field because nobody traveled long distances by foot. I associated the dead walkers (milkmaids, cowherds) with my own home because of all the old stuff inside it, which could have been touched by their dead hands, and also because I knew them from television, which was the place where I saw living people wearing old-fashioned clothing, and which had given my mind's eye the time-lapse sequences that tumbled through my head when I looked at the holly trees and saw a restfulness that I found difficult to imagine. They had stayed in the same place since the day they were planted. On the reel in my mind's eye bent-shouldered people flickered past them, the moon scudded overhead, the wind howled through the branches, the sun paused at the zenith on a hot still day, the roots dried in the parched earth, deer browsed and vanished, snow dusted the tiny valleys between prickles on the leaves, a gliding owl's belly brushed the topmost prong, the light rose and clouded over, the bark slowly healed over the tooth marks, day and night flickered on and off, on and off again, and the trees never went anywhere. They were no more, nor less present during the night than the day.

The school bus pulled over that slope each morning. The road cut over the hill on a very short, very steep stretch that rose from a T-junction where the bed-and-breakfast stood. The slope was short and steep. There was one driver who would never shift gear. Each morning we would be moving steadily along and then as we reached the sign warning the pitched angle of the upcoming slope I'd start to feel the sensation of tipping upward, the weight in my body pushing into the back of the chair. The bus nosed itself up the steep curve and began to climb. I could feel the huge old wheels rumbling round slower and more slowly as the speed decreased, until we were nearly at the top of the hill and almost at a standstill, the whole huge metal framework dragging its weight, and that of the bodies inside it, forward inch by slow inch. I could see the driver hunched over his huge wheel. As a passenger I had the feeling that he just wasn't trying, but I could see that his foot was fully down on the accelerator and there was no purchase. We were only a few meters from the peak when the expected lurch came, a feeling of having left my insides a few inches in front of me as the bus halted, quite still for one moment, in the pause between inhale and exhale, and then lurched downward. The driver slammed the brake and ground through the change in gear he should have made at the bottom of the slope. The movement downward was only a pang or a twinge, the bus came into gear and noisily dragged its weight over the peak.

I anticipated this moment as I approached the slope and in the pause between going up and going down I was filled with a certainty that this would be the day we'd roll back down to the junction and smash through the walls of the bed-and-breakfast at the bottom.

The same thing happened every day and yet this didn't diminish its physical tension. On the way home, rolling downward, I didn't even notice the hill. But it was when we were rolling downhill, with a different driver, on a winter afternoon when the sky was already darkening and it wasn't yet four, there had been heavy rain that day and then the temperature dropped and it must have frozen the water, thick and invisible, on the road, because we rolled down the hill without hesitating at the stop sign and kept on rolling. It was only a few seconds and it all felt very calm. The bus cruised, not especially quickly. The driver said "Whoa" with muted surprise, as though he had accidentally discovered a new function on his game console. In one movement the bus crossed the road and hurtled toward the wall of the building, and the driver pressed the button so that the doors hissed open. He sprang up out of his seat to throw himself free, only, in the last second, turning back to yank the steering wheel almost as an afterthought, as his body pulled away from it. The bus swerved around the corner and up the road, which slowed it down. The driver held the wheel and the bus continued to turn, so that its nose was in the bed-and-breakfast's small parking lot by the time he pulled on the hand brake. In the quiet that followed, Ash's dad emerged from the building. It wasn't his usual working hours. He had a pencil behind his ear and a hammer in his hand. He addressed the driver through the open doors in a friendly but disinterested voice. "I can think of better ways to get rid of them."

A few times a year, when my father and I went mushrooming or walking together, he would bring his huge ocher gardening mitt, black from engine oil on the fingertips, and a carrier bag. As we returned down the hill toward our house he would collect litter from the verge. At three points along this verge there were slumps of dirty sand and gravel which were used in winter for gritting the road, each one dented by rainfall into the form of a volcano. The litter somehow drifted against and often half-embedded itself in these dumps so that they came to look like ugly plants, sprouting chocolate-bar wrappers from which the decoration and brand name had washed away, leaving only a silver slip with the original colors in its deepest creases, and plastic bottles, and aluminum cans slowly filling with grit. It was as though there was some controlling force that was trying to separate human effects from the plants on the verges—grasses, earth, cow parsley, hawthorn hedge—and the human element didn't come out of it looking good. Insects connected the different zones, feeding off the litter's sticky bits or gathering on the dusty stalks of the roadside plants. Occasionally I kept a piece of litter if I liked the look of it: a small but heavy green glass bottle; a smooth piece of marbled plastic. There was an orange ring pull, I think from a limited-edition Fanta, and recently I saw this same ring pull in an image of a dead seabird. The bird's wings are spread as though she is floating above the world, but she is down on the ground. Beside her, on a beautiful rock whose surface is decorated with lichens in shades of primrose and duck egg, there is an array of manufactured objects and parts, which are at the same time alien and intimately familiar. The objects were found inside the bird's corpse. An orange tab placed beside the elegant bend of the bird's neck. I had last seen that tab twenty years earlier, arranged with some other rubbish on the concrete in my backyard. It had traveled many thousands and thousands of miles and made its way into the entrails of this bird that had died somewhere along the northern coast of Chile. At the beginning of lockdown there were stories all over the news about how ecosystems were recovering in the absence of humans—a pair of falcons nesting in Times Square, a bear cub padding through urban streets in Akita, okapi in Kinshasa, weeds flowering on the walls of the Bank of England. Most of these sightings were found to be fakes but there had always been something fairy-tale about them, exposing nothing so much as the storyteller's desire that healing could be quick and painless. Meanwhile particles of plastic from packets I opened when I was a child are circulating, right now, through the bodies of newly hatched birds.

I never saw anybody else collecting the litter, it set us apart from the other people who lived in the area. A few years ago, during a break from work on a communal farm in Cornwall, I was sitting with a group of seasonal laborers in a barn, on a circle of hay bales, eating the fried eggs and sliced white toast that were provided for our lunch. I'd been pinching out tomatoes in the polytunnel with the man now sitting next to me who had told me that he stayed, year-round, in a yurt in the orchard. As we ate I asked him where he had lived before he came to the farm. I had assumed, without really thinking about it, that my question was banal—a silence-breaker, a form of disarmament. In response the man told me that his parents ran a garden center near a beltway outside Gloucester. After he spoke, the man sitting on the other side of him flinched and turned away and the other farmworkers who were near enough to hear looked at their feet. The sentence, as this man voiced it, trembled with distaste for Gloucester, for parents, for beltways and for garden centers, and it was clear that he could hardly contain some huge and inexplicable rage at the persistence of these specific phenomena. I guessed the communal biodynamic farm, where human life organized itself around a shared respect for vegetables, grains, and moon cycles, contained his rage for him, and I changed the subject. Since then I have noticed how expressions of care for the environment are often outlets for hatred of other humans, both in the accusation that *we* are bad for other species, in which the accuser rarely seems to understand themselves to be a part of any *we*, and also in the protection of a privileged experience of greenery over the voices and essential needs of the poorer indigenous and local people. In England, the phrase *local people* is a byword for a community that is corrupted by its ignorance and incest—not only poor and under-educated, but repellently so.

My father wasn't one of those people who collect litter as an expression of hatred for the people who create it, but what we were doing was still a mark of our own considerable self-respect, which expressed itself in love for our surroundings, the weedy verges and the interconnected collection of stories that was told by the holly trees which straggled out of the hedge to mark the disused path. They were haunted by a bent figure whose face was concealed by her thin, rough-edged, dun-colored shawl. She struggled, lost, through deep snowdrifts, and then discovered with relief the dark green prickly-leaved beacon ahead. Her surprise and relief moved into my body. Seen across the landscape, the trees unfolded a path and their hedge, seen across time, remembered the past. Hedges were everywhere but they were usually the divisions between things rather than things in themselves: brown background against which my own figure could shine.

At school, the substitute teacher disappeared and Ms. Carr returned. As we filed past her into assembly one morning, Ann asked about the baby and Ms. Carr replied with a gentle smile. Sadly, the baby had been born too early and had not survived. Ms. Carr looked older than ever. She was thin again—it seemed impossible that she could have carried a pregnancy. She had her arm in a sling. I guess we all assumed that was something to do with the baby too. I was still in Mrs. Hepton's class. At that time I rarely spoke to Clare and hardly ever went out to the quarry, in which four new mustard-colored machines were busy. The track at the top had been turned into a proper road and there was nowhere for me to sit because the dump truck roared along it several times a day. Sometimes the man in the cabin was Dmitri, who was working longer days at a faster pace. Because there were houses on the top field, the quarry couldn't grow any wider, and so the base dropped deeper and deeper, the earth down there became dark and dense. I didn't see sand martins or kestrels there while the work was going on—too noisy—but the place itself felt more, not less, alive. A new aggression came over it. Things I had always seen took on new meanings. The green van with the slats in the side, animal noses poking through to taste fresh air as they were taken away. Bruised cheekbones, arms in plaster casts. Smashed glass and one red spot on the pavement outside the pub the morning after payday. The only violence I had noticed, up to that point, had been staged by Rebecca.

Rebecca lived in an area in the far corner of the village. I didn't often go to her house, I wasn't much invited. There was a nursing home surrounded by a high wall, a paddock with two horses and two ponies in it, and a mossy lane leading to Rebecca's cottage. Rebecca's mother ran the small local hospital and Rebecca's father had been a surgeon at a larger hospital in the city, but then suddenly he stopped and started working as the gardener at the nursing home. The lane they lived on was exceptionally pretty. The ground was covered with short grass and moss, with tall chalky-brick walls on either side. At one end, this wall concealed their garden. A white lilac tree overhung it there, and in late spring its scent dropped down to fill the narrow lane as a bath fills with water. At the other end of the path ivy had grown thickly over the wall. Tentacles hung down, filtering sunlight. That end of the lane also smelled good, but the ivy scent was peppery and dusty. Inside the ivy I had once found a nest with three blue eggs inside it. The outside was rough and twiggy, the central dimple as smooth as if it had been molded from clay. I came back every day that spring and witnessed the eggs turn into two small gelid creatures, and then loud fluffy chicks which puffed up, eventually, to blackbirds. I saw them practicing fledging, sidestepping, wobbly, along the old ivy stalk, and I missed their flying off. The nest remained empty after that, though I always checked it if I happened to walk down that lane, and deliberately dulled my footfall as I approached. At the end, the lane opened out into a small field, bisected by a plastic white ribbon, in which there lived the two horses and two ponies who were owned by Rebecca's family.

One day I crept along the last part of the lane, peeped into the nest, empty, and then, slipping through the gate, I scared the huge horse, who was standing close by. He kicked his back legs high as he startled and ran off, and the hoof went right into my face, stopping a millimeter in front of me. I thought: that would have killed me. I didn't blink, the image imprinted itself in my mind. The hoof was huge and the horseshoe half concealed by impacted dirt. It took up most of my field of vision and I couldn't see the leg behind it—it was suspended in front of me like a planet in space.

Behind the wall, on the other side of the lane, was the nursing home for the elderly, where Ash's mom worked, and Rebecca's dad was the gardener. Before that it had been a maternity hospital (my father was born there), but all the children of the community knew that the house had ghosts because the man who had built it had died in the First World War, before he ever moved in.

Rebecca's father was visible in the grounds of this dead house whenever I passed by. He wore sandy-colored denim overalls on his body; on his face he wore the light but definite look of disappointment. His lawn dropped away below the terrace with a short, sharp slope, whose tidy perfection told me that it had not been created for me to roll on it; for any form of play. Around the lawn were borders in which there were straight ranks of flowers in flat colors, organized in stripes or regular repeating patterns. Rebecca's father must have been ruthless about browned petals and drooping foliage because the beds were forever bright. Behind them, above a dry, red-brown dust, there were cedar trees which screened off the high wall above the road, which created a background of blue-green shade whose empty depths offset the bright foreground.

It was unexpected therefore to walk over the terrace and look in at the window to find not a young lady in a white dress practicing the piano, but padded chairs with armrests on which plastic meal trays were fixed, all turned to focus on a massive television. In making his ugly old-fashioned garden, Rebecca's father wasn't trying to re-create the gardens of the house's past, but the gardens that had been fashionable at the time when the people who lived in the nursing home were young.

Rebecca's home was the house that families move to English villages for: mellow stone, fat roses, lawn. Her parents had a car each. I liked it there, but Rebecca and her younger sister Sara didn't come out as much as the other children in the village did. They were reserved—shy, I think, more than superior, but it's difficult, even as an adult, to be generous enough to make that distinction and I wasn't inclined to at the time. Rebecca rarely volunteered to talk at school and when she was directly addressed, either by the teacher or at playtime, she would respond in short, clipped sentences, as though reluctant to spend her thoughts. It didn't help that she was glorious, physically—tall and substantial with smooth, honey-colored skin, dark brown eyes, a slight plumpness that spoke of self-satisfaction.

Occasionally Rebecca and Sara invited some of the other children in the village, myself included, to come over to play in their paddling pool, which was one of those high-sided plastic pools that is almost a proper swimming pool. Or they would want to share some new thing they had—Rollerblades or something recently released by Nintendo. These objects never quite worked within a group. The footwear didn't fit, or the console was set up for two players, and so there was more time waiting between turns than there was for playing, and more often than not, the toys made actual fun impossible. I didn't truly enjoy going to Rebecca's house. I was invited because my jealousy increased Rebecca's appreciation of what she had, rather than because she wanted to share her pleasure. Obviously I didn't think that at the time—my feelings for new products were intense. I was happy just to be in their presence.

Then one day Rebecca invited Ann and me over after school but when we arrived, there was nothing new. It was late autumn, the playground gear was wet and grubby with sodden leaves and the screens inside the house were all black. In the kitchen, Rebecca stood proudly beside Sara, her neck long and her hands folded: responsible and pleased. The two sisters' faces were very different— Sara's thin and pointed, Rebecca's broad and masculine—but they shared streams of long, fine, gold-brown hair, brushed in preparation for our arrival, the flyaway tips attaching themselves to one another with electricity.

Their mother poured out cranberry juice and Ann and I stood awkwardly, sipping it, then quickly sipping again, until the mother left. Rebecca watched the door close and then turned back.

"We are moving to Australia," she said quickly, in an affectedly formal, adult voice. "My mother has a great new job there."

The cranberry juice carton was standing on the counter beyond Rebecca's floating hair. I'd never tasted it before. There was a picture of a blue wave crashing on the side of the packet and I could feel that wave, precisely the same size as the wave on the carton, crashing in my mouth. Everything was deliciously sweet with a bitter edge that made it clean. Rebecca went on about Australia. Their house there was painted blue. She and Sara would see koalas and kangaroos. I could see these animals processing through the garden of a blue cottage, and, overlaid, I could see Sara in the kitchen, her eyes switching from my face to Ann's, drinking in our responses.

At school we heard more about Australia as the departure approached. In the cold, bleak months after Christmas, Rebecca talked about the huge clear skies. When spring began she talked about how she and Sara would be free to gallop on their horses for miles through wild landscapes like nothing we had ever known.

I didn't believe it: they didn't do much galloping in the village, only, occasionally, bobbing in velvet-covered hats along the lane and back. But that didn't stop me feeling Rebecca's longing. There was something inspired about her in those final days as she explained to me, more and more frantically, how much better things would be in Australia. She had a new, indefinite freedom, talking in long splurging stories, where previously she had been reticent. She looked older, too. It was visible, through her shirt, that she was wearing a training bra.

After school, in those long evenings of the longest days of the year, Rebecca started playing out and she brought Sara along with her, though Sara was never quite comfortable engaging with the long, physical, loosely organized games the rest of us played. They were leaving at the beginning of the summer holidays. The departure approached. Australia receded from the stories as Rebecca became preoccupied with the journey. On one of her last days we found ourselves lying on the roof of the garden shed, at the back of the new estate, hiding from some boys during a war game. I was trying to make Rebecca be quiet as she talked and talked about her suitcase with a rainbow-colored belt, about how you got free drinks on the airplane, and first-class seats reclined almost to beds.

Then they left. There were blinds over their windows and a FOR SALE sign outside. I climbed into their garden once, just to make the point, but there was no thrill—it felt evacuated and neutral. When I walked along the lane I pulled on a tentacle of the ivy and it came away, catching and jerking, in one long thread, pulling out bits of wall as it did so, so that I showered white grainy mortar onto my own head. If I kept pulling, I felt that the wall would come down.

The summer passed and it was nearly time to return to school when I climbed on that wall outside to drop down into the lane. From the top of the wall I could see into the nursing home garden. There, framed by cedar branches, bending over the fading flowerbeds, was Rebecca's father. It was unmistakably him. He was wearing the pale brown denim overalls he always wore. I jumped, and ran to the end of the lane to look. The FOR SALE sign had come down outside the house. The blinds had rolled up and there were two new cars on the gravel.

When I walked in through the school gates for the first day back at school, I noticed Mrs. Hepton's potted plants, still standing in a row in the playground. I thought for a strange moment that they had been doused with bleach or acid. The wide surfaces of the leaves had blanched irregularly, almost to white. Others were a sickly lurid green. The plants had thinned and drooped through six weeks of long northern summer days, standing in full sunlight. They needed shade. Mrs. Hepton returned her burnt plants to the far end of the classroom, away from the windows. Some of them recovered, partially.

Rebecca and Sara were also back. They hadn't missed a single day of school. When we asked them why they had returned from Australia, they only gave vague answers: their mother didn't like the job, their father "didn't get on" with the climate. I guessed that they didn't know the reason. Maybe there was no good reason, maybe the whole thing was a parental whim. Anyway, Rebecca and Sara were even more reserved after that. I can't remember being invited to their house again, though they were still living there when I left. Rebecca, in particular, seemed to have been marked by the event— she carried the family's aborted migration, as the eldest child often carries the whole family's burden of a wrenching change. She jolted as though stung when addressed in class, reddening, and offering a response angrily, as though inviting her to speak was a form of assault. At break she played only with her sister.

The next time she spoke to me I was in the lane outside her house at lilac time again. The ivy inside which the bird had nested had been cleared, leaving dried white rootlets which traced veins and spiders' legs on the bricks. Rebecca was sitting under the tree, on shade-dappled moss. She was bending over something and I approached, tentatively. I wanted to see what the new thing was.

Rebecca leaned back to show me. It was a broken starling lying star-shaped, its wings tormented into reversals of their natural form. It croaked in response to each quick, sure stab or twist made by Rebecca, who had a metal barbecue skewer in her hand. She moved in a deft and particular way, as though she was conducting an experiment or medical operation, and her expression was fascinated and serious. She was breathing heavily as she performed her surgery. The starling's breast was leopard-spotted and the feathers gleamed as though they had been doused in petrol. They parted irregularly, like cracks in an ice sheet, to reveal glimpses of thin white skin right down at the bottom of the feather ravine. The wing feathers were slim and filmy; individual feathers had been pushed out of place at intervals by Rebecca, to make a pretty regular pattern. We sat in the close-cropped grass, in a cloud of lilac scent, with Rebecca's cottage behind it, my head touching hers so that we could both get close. She had shifted over a little and patted the grass beside her: she wanted me to share it. The starling was spot-lit by a circle of light that fell between the lilac's heart-shaped leaves. I wondered whether it would feel different if she was doing the same things to a worm. There has to be a point at which suffering becomes so diminished as an experience that I don't need to take it seriously. The starling's small and easily manipulable body was compelling: was it a machine, responding to the press of a button, or were we in the presence of agony? Simple animals connect people to objects but the connection is disruptive and children aren't stupid: I knew instinctively that cruelty scales up to blossom in the adult. It was obvious that the experience that Rebecca was having was sexual. The violence was a by-product, as it usually is. Slow violence, systemic violence, remote violence, residues of most human processes, are the most widely generated by-products of my lifetime and hers. In my late twenties I was living on-and-off in Texas and I was surprised to hear a new perspective on local radio one baking spring morning. The house that I stayed in had a small yard, and I sat every morning on the rotting wooden steps that led out into it, though I never, over the months and then years that I stayed there, stepped out onto the dusty brown ivy that completely covered the ground. I drank my weak American coffee, watching two grackles squabbling, feeling the heat on my face, and I could hear the weatherman's faint voice reading out the temperature from behind the screen door. There was a heat wave. His Texan voice read out the temperature in Dallas, El Paso, Houston, San Antonio, which meant nothing to me because I don't understand Fahrenheit. "Phew," he said. "It's hot! But we'll push that temperature a little bit higher by noon."

I loved Texas and was very happy there. One of the things that impressed me was the troubling and unusual way the Texans took responsibility for their own destructive behavior. When I drove from one city to another the cattle businesses went on for miles and miles of churned earth and shit, running seamlessly to the horizon, the fug of dung pervading the inside of the car, with hundreds and hundreds, then thousands and thousands, of cream and brown cattle standing quite still at the railing beside the freeway, streaming across the window. I drove and the cattle continued. Minutes passed. Still the cattle thronged the side of the road, and at some point, I became unable to think of the bodies as living individuals.

The heat was baking but the earth never hardened or cracked under their feet, they stood forever knee-deep in wet shit that receded behind them as far as the eye could see. Some weeks later I met a rancher at a drinks reception I had been invited to for work. I asked him about all these cows and how many he, personally, owned. He replied by telling me not the number of cattle but the volume of living beef, in tons, on his ranch. In Texas I enjoyed talking to people who were quite comfortable in understanding themselves as violent and self-seeking creatures. They pushed up the temperature and they owned it; they welcomed competition and loved their weapons; they believed in war as the route to peace; and this ability to live with themselves was, to me, undeniably wholesome.

ONE DAY MY MOTHER PICKED me up from school and we went in the car to the stately home a few miles from the village, following the road that went past Rebecca's house. My mother paid the entrance fee for the grounds only and we walked along the path for miles. The garden was bigger than some farms. We had been there a few times before. This time, my mother had a camera with her and she paused to take photographs of every feature and new perspective that came into view. A spreading tree, a tiny fake ruined castle, a small dome with pillars around it set on the top of a miniature hill.

I stood in the foreground and beamed for these photographs until eventually, with only a hint of a smile, my mother told me that she was taking slides for a class that she was teaching on old gardens. The pictures of me might make the course less boring for her students, but perhaps I didn't need to be in every single one.

That weekend we went out in the car again, driving farther this time. I fell asleep in the car and woke up as we turned in at a gatehouse, approaching a huge grey building I hadn't been to before. This house had an intimidating look: it was asymmetrical, with many pointy bits of roof and a large glasshouse like an iceberg on the side.

We parked on the gravel and walked right up to the house. My mother knocked on a side door, which was answered by one of the strangest-looking women I had ever seen.

She was tiny, not much taller than I was, pale, with a bony face, a large nose, and small eyes behind huge plastic glasses. Her head tilted as she looked at us, like a bird's. Her hair, straws of grey, white, and brown, was pulled back with an elastic band, and she was dressed like a farmer—men's corduroy trousers and a man's shirt—except for the huge diamond earrings that dragged on her earlobes. "Darling," she said, shortly. She leaned toward my mother as though to kiss, but turned her head aside, fractionally, at the last moment, so that the kisses landed on air.

We walked straight into a huge kitchen. The radio was on. There were two younger women sitting at the far end of a long table. They greeted my mother, and she greeted them familiarly. The two women were both very good-looking. One of them said that she had better get back to work, and she turned to some pots and pans on the old-fashioned black range.

"You don't want a coffee," said the strange woman to my mother, definitively. My mother shook her head. Then the woman fixed me with her eyes.

"You can call me Ruth," she said in a loud, distinct voice.

We left the kitchen by another door and walked along corridors until we came out in a large hallway with a wide wooden staircase.

Through the door I could see a room the height of the whole building with bookshelves reaching to the roof, and a gallery above so
that you could browse the high shelves. We turned into a side room,
shuttered off. Ruth switched on the light. It was cold. The chill, the
shutters, and the bare, bright electric bulb had a sad feeling. Ruth
turned to a row of paintings on the wall.

"This is it," she said. "What I decided is that these two must be
the same man—Kasumi's put them together for you. See the nose."

We all looked at two portraits of two men, wearing two different
outfits. The men did not look similar to me but they both had a
broken nose, large and triangular.

"We've had the girl from Bonham's here," said Ruth to my
mother. "She said it might help with verification. So I don't need
your advice, just thought you'd be interested."

She turned back to look at the two pictures of the men.

My mother broke the silence. "Was one of these the marriage
portrait? Where is Anna?"

"She's so fucking ugly," said Ruth. "I've put her upstairs."

I looked at the paintings on the wall. There was a row of portraits,
five or so, each one showing a substantial, pale-skinned person in
elaborate clothing. Each subject of each portrait was arrestingly
ugly. I looked at them for a long time and the people inside the pictures held my gaze. They looked bored.

On the adjacent wall there was a larger painting of three
children. Ruth turned to this painting, and then looked down at
me. She pointed to the painting, and addressed me in the same loud,
distinct way that she had before. "Do you think these are girls, then,
or boys?"

The children in the painting had long white curls and silk frilled dresses—one pink, one blue, one white.

"Girls," I said.

"Ha!" said Ruth. "They are boys." She bent down toward me. "Little boys had to wear dresses in those days." She walked out of the room, chuckling to herself.

The annex at the top of the house was in a state of degradation, even compared to the other rooms. We were high up inside the roof and there were windows which made me think of onions, round, deep-set into the wall, with the paint around them loose and peeling away. I leaned over and picked at the thick paint and it was heavy with mold and moisture, lifting away from the surface.

"The flat's a disaster," said Ruth. "I've sold some houses in the village to pay for it and now they're all threatening to shoot me."

My mother began to ask a question about the tenants in the village and Ruth stopped her with an abrupt gesture of her hands, like a conductor silencing an orchestra.

"I've given this place my entire life," she said. "No doubt," she said acidly, "Simon will implement conscientious new policies. He has to wait until I croak."

The fucking ugly painting we were looking for was hanging on the corridor wall. The subject looked exhausted. Her face was unusual—distinctive: she looked, in fact, not unlike Ruth, though her facial expression was more vacuous. In the corner of her portrait there was a dark-skinned child who looked directly out at me with a steady gaze which hovered with the vital and lively force the woman lacked.

We looked at the painting for a moment. My mother frowned but said nothing. The corridor appeared to lead to a dead end, but when Ruth fiddled with the wall, a hidden door sprung open. Behind it there was a narrow, dark staircase with bobbles of fluff and cobwebs on the bare boards. Ruth gestured upward. "Please."

I walked up behind her, stroking the grainy wooden banister, and when I came out into the light there were circles of matte grey dust on my fingertips, and we were standing on the roof. Sheets of dark metal were laid out, making mazy paths between the slated grey slopes. We walked around them, through the rooftops, until we could see down, three stories, to the terrace, the lawns, and their large trees. Ruth bent down to address me again.

"The lead paths were made for the women of the house," she said. "So that they could walk up here and never had to go outside, where men might get them."

She stepped right up to the edge, her toes almost curling over the drop, and her whole body trembled like a stem in the breeze.

Following her gaze, I looked down on the cypress tree that was growing on the edge of the lawn. In the crown, where its two main branches parted, there was a beautiful, large, pale grey pigeon, edging in side steps along a twig. The pigeon took off and landed in the next tree, a huge copper beech, its leaves spreading and rustling like old dresses the color of black plums. The pigeon disappeared inside the dark foliage, the branch bouncing behind it, and then suddenly a magpie burst out through the leaves, croaked once, and landed on a television aerial that had been taped onto the side of a roof.

When I turned back, Ruth was looking at me. She addressed my mother. "He doesn't say much."

"Get her on the right subject," my mother replied in her mild voice, "and she won't shut up."

Ruth scrutinized me for a moment, then shrugged, as though giving up on a pointless argument.

"You want to see the garden," she told us.

There was a gardener in the walled garden, half concealed inside a border that was frothy with tall flowers. We walked past a huge henhouse which was a miniature version of the main house, except, on the inside walls, somebody had painted magnificent bare-breasted women, some with fishtails, others combing their hair, wearing shells or pearls, or trailing seaweed which covered or revealed their nakedness. "Suzie's thing," said Ruth. "Bit camp."

She marched us around the different gardens inside the garden, barking out the Latin names of the plants and informing us as to whether they were thriving or weak. Then we went into the hothouse.

The door closed behind us and we were in another world. It was an old building, the roof domed, the thin metal-framed panes glazed with trickling moisture. The plants arched above and around us, prehistoric, and I wouldn't have been surprised to see a beady eye or scaly tail or long golden feather flick and disappear.

These plants were labeled with small white placards on plastic sticks that had been pushed into the damp compost. The Latin names of the plants meant nothing to me but I had heard of their places of origin: Barbados, Trinidad, Carolina, Florida, Georgia. Some olden person had annotated these labels in looped handwriting with notes on the environment that the original seed, cutting, or entire plant had been lifted from: forest, mountain, swamp, plantation.

Ruth, meanwhile, had pulled a pale grey silk handkerchief out of her pocket and flitted around the room like a hummingbird, tenderly wiping a leaf here, turning a pot there, and, all the while, murmuring questions in a soft voice which was entirely different from that which she had used with us. "Why are you flowering already, little one? What are you doing under here?"

While she had her back turned and was facing away from me, absorbed in her leaves and tendrils, I lifted one placard out of the nearest pot and pocketed it. When I ran my fingers over it, I could feel that there were words picked in relief on the underside of the placard, where the plastic stalk met the back of the label, but I didn't dare bring it out to look at what it said.

The two beautiful women were still sitting in the kitchen, at the end of the long table, talking. One was dark-skinned, with a long plait, and the other pale, with loose fair hair. They introduced themselves to me: Kasumi and Suzanna. The adults conferred for a moment, and then Kasumi asked me if I would like to make drop-scones on the hot plate.

"Yes," I said.

My mother told me that she had some work to do with Ruth and they left.

While they were gone I stayed with the two women. We poured tiny pancakes directly onto the hot stone and then the three of us played snakes and ladders on an old board which was torn along one quarter. The radio was talking quietly the whole time, the kitchen was warm and it smelled of batter. I asked the women who they were. Kasumi told me that she worked as a housekeeper. Then the two women exchanged glances and I had the bizarre impression that they felt vulnerable in my presence. Suzanna turned her large blue eyes to look at me.

"I'm Ruth's girlfriend," she said, "and I am a painter."

We had lunch. The adults drank wine and talked about people I didn't know, laughing, on and off, all the way through the meal. Kasumi joined us at first, but as soon as she had finished her food she rose abruptly and said, "Right then." She hung an apron around her neck and left the room. I didn't see her again. Mostly, I concentrated on my food, which was good—pasta with herbs and cream—but Ruth pierced my train of thought when she raised her voice to declare:

"I do whatever the fuck I like because I don't care what people think."

Suzanna, whose cheekbones had dots of pink on them, waved her fork in the air:

"No," she said. "You can do whatever the fuck you like because you have this place."

Ruth smiled in a patronizing way and rolled her eyes.

"Seriously, though," said Suzanna. Her fork was still raised. "There aren't many people who can afford to not care what people think."

Ruth chuckled and turned to me. "Here we go," she said. I was tired on the way home. When I tried to lie down in the back seat of the car, something poked into my side. I felt in my pocket, and drew out the plastic plant label. I read the raised lettering that was printed in relief along the back: *Made in China*.

I said, "Why did we go to that place?"

My mother said, "Ruth is our cousin."

"I see," I said.

I CAN'T REMEMBER A TIME when Clare began to be ill. It happened in an ongoing way, in the way that most things happened and still happen: without attachment to date or hour, in a suspended present—hovering. It's not that I was unaware of time. A few spaces were marked out with conventional linearity, the obvious example would be the classroom. During the last half hour of the school day my body was aware of clock time in the way a predator is aware of its quarry:

my body, following it, absorbed its pace and direction of movement. Clare went bald. I remember going into her house and her not being there because she was in the hospital, and there was another time when she was in her bedroom and then out again, recovering on the sofa. I remember looking through the open door on a hot day and seeing her lying on the sofa with the curtains drawn. Her face was made of hollows and shadows and she was cackling, with her manly, provocative laugh, at some innovative violence on Nickelodeon. I stood in the doorway, shifting from foot to foot, no more awkward than I had been before. "Is Adam playing?" I asked.

I do not know much about where Clare went or what she experienced but I can describe how her sickness reshaped the environment she left behind. At school there was a power vacuum and the girl who ascended to the top of the hierarchy was not a director in Clare's image but a caring, round-faced girl named Jane, a farmer's daughter who already looked like the overstretched mother she would soon become. At playtime the girls collectively deferred to Jane, who gently suggested unimaginative role-plays involving families and poorly animals. Meanwhile Adam, who was in the year below me, gained an uneasy popularity. He was small for his age and quiet, and he'd previously had only one close friend, but when Clare became ill everybody wanted to sit next to him or pick him first for the team, whatever the game was. In the summer when there were school fêtes and sports days, all charities were forgotten other than the charity of the local children's ward. Every cause we had ever supported receded beyond the pale: Clare's illness narrowed the world's suffering to a fine, hyperlocal point. Save the Whales, I had written on the posters I made at school. Save the Rainforests. These were vague messages, sent out without direction, like a message in a bottle. They were instructions rather than intentions: I wasn't planning to do any saving myself. Now we needed to save Clare and naturally we had no faith in our own ability to do it locally. Children gravely discussed treatment options in America or London. Eventually, in the playground, the fact that Clare would die came to be accepted with equanimity. We had grown up with meat farms.

Yesterday my friend Kay emailed and asked if we could have a video call and I told her that I could do any day, any time. When we spoke this afternoon, Kay asked me how I was doing, in isolation, but I could see that she was distracted. Her children were visible in the background of my screen, climbing on the back of the sofa. I called hello to them and they froze, then came up very close to the camera and peered at me. "Where's Granny?"

"We're not talking to Granny right now," said Kay, and she lifted her laptop off the table and carried it over to the other side of the room, explaining to me about her work timetable and nursery provision for essential workers. I found it difficult to follow her but I didn't say anything, I knew it would be over before long—parents adore to describe their childcare arrangements and I knew from experience that if I didn't sit patiently through the part of the conversation that was relentlessly focused on the offspring, we would never escape through the other side, to different subjects, the wider world. Kay switched on the television and the children sat down in front of it. Then she took her laptop into her bedroom and closed the door. "Joe's gone," she said.

I didn't respond. Kay had told me, a year earlier, that she and her boyfriend had run out of conversation, so much so that she had started to hate going out for dinner with him. There was nothing to say to one another and the silence between them embarrassed her. She felt that it exposed something ugly and dull about them, chewing like dumb animals together. At the time I'd tried to comfort her by comparing them to cattle. I thought that there was something tender about eating in silence together as I had seen the cattle do when I was a child. It's rare to have a companion whose presence is enough, and anyway, there is no person who is so fascinatingly alive that they are never interested in what's on their plate.

This afternoon on the video call I apologized for saying that. I shouldn't have compared her to an animal. Kay laughed and said that she couldn't remember that conversation. They'd had an argument. "Not good," she said. "Physical."

I asked her if she was safe and she said "Mm," not looking into the camera. "Actually it was mostly me."

The difficult thing was explaining to the children that she didn't know where their father was. She'd called everybody she could think of. "Maybe in a hotel"—Joseph earned good money—"but hotels are closed." She frowned slightly. "What's that noise?"

I listened but I couldn't hear anything unusual. Then I realized that it was the sound of my smoke alarm beeping. The battery had run out and they never seemed to be in stock when I ordered my grocery delivery. I'd grown used to the sound of the beeping. "You need to disconnect it," said Kay. "That shit can drive you mad."

"Maybe it's time to call the police," I said.

After we had finished talking I disconnected my alarm.

It was in winter, when Clare was ill, that I had started to help with the cattle on Mr. Gray's farm. He invited me, after seeing me creeping around buildings in the open barnyard or climbing in the haystack. The invitation seemed strange to me at the time, he would have worked more quickly without me there, but I was aware that he wanted to prolong the life of the thing he loved, as adults often do. The child, the gene, is not the end but the means. Mr. Gray said that I could call him Thomas but not Tom, on the whole he preferred Mr. Gray. I never felt scared of him. I felt in fact that he was scared of me, especially when I attempted to initiate one of my polite conversations.

The cows lived in cramped circumstances but they created a huge calm space inside this small enclosure and they made it out of sheer mood. The herd had a genius for tolerance. Its members were regularly disappeared. At that time I had a strong experience of relief when I was inside this space, where the quietness was amplified by communal chewing and slow breathing. The first time I went in, it was of course the bull I noticed. As soon as Mr. Gray and I entered the barn, the bull separated himself from the herd and approached the barrier, and Mr. Gray went to meet him and scratch his nose. He wore black rubber gloves that were similar in texture to the bull's nose, which tilted slightly up and down with what looked like mild pleasure as the scratching went on, for a minute or two. Watching it, I felt that this courtly and formal exchange seemed to show that the bull was fond of the farmer, but there was an apprehensiveness to it, some motivation of condescension or fear which the bull could not or would not manifest in a way that communicated to humans. When the bull returned to his cows Mr. Gray took a rusty knife to the black plastic silage bale. He drew a long line along the top with the blunt blade, the plastic split, and the bale sprang apart in bound slices, and then it was our job, his and mine, to carry these slices to the feeder. He handled them with ease, as though they weighed nothing, but they were heavy to me, I had to carry them on my shoulder and catapult them into the trough. This process was imprecise, I dropped straw on the floor to the side of the trough and Mr. Gray wordlessly scraped it up and put it in the right place. My technique hardly improved with time.

One day, levering a poorly balanced load, I pronged the bull on the nose with my pitchfork. He backed away slowly, moving his hooves without looking behind him, and waited for me to back away too. After that, he was always circumspect with me. He eyed my movements and made room around my end of the trough as I approached. Mr. Gray told me that the bull couldn't distinguish between me and the pitchfork—that something in a cow's eyes means that it doesn't see that there is a border between a body and any implement that body happens to be holding. This made sense to me. I could see why the pitchfork-child hybrid would alarm the bull and it didn't make me admire him any less. He was undeniably the most important person in the barn. I have heard that born leaders have a special aura when you glimpse them in real life—that you sense that the leader is looking directly at you, wherever you are in relation to one another in a space. The bull was like that. If he batted his head to one side the cows would scatter. When he lowed, a gentle sound which seemed to originate in his hips, the others followed suit, and they turned from him and dipped their heads as signs of deference. I didn't share their desire to devote their lives to him but I could understand why they felt that way—his size was awesome, his huge neck, wider than his head, was both solid and soft, and covered with clean shining curls. What made him appealing was the fact that this huge body was animated and contained by an immense gentleness. During foddering he stood a few steps back from the feeding trough, nudging the little cows around so that they all had their turn. Eventually, only after they had been eating for a while, he created a space for himself at the center and began to eat, and ate, and was usually still eating when I left. It seemed incredible that this huge being could sustain itself on dry grass. I once asked Mr. Gray the bull's name, and he told me that the bull was registered as 49327100 G-R-A-Y. "He's the only bull, he doesn't need a name." But the cows had names and over time I came to know them as individuals.

One morning, in the middle of feeding, a small cow started screaming. I turned to look. Physically unremarkable, patched ginger and cream. She was elongating her back and tensing her chin forward, thrusting her tongue out with the effort of it. Mr. Gray turned to look at me but I shrugged. I was on the far side of the barn, it couldn't have been me. He turned back to the cow and murmured something in a calm voice but she only became more agitated. The scream was so piercing that it was a sensation of touch rather than sound, I could feel it vibrating inside the trunk of my body. This disruption—my feeling her presence inside me—was what she wanted. Eventually Mr. Gray and I left the barn and then she stopped. It happened again the next day. That was Ivy.

Ivy was unlike the other cows. She was no good at living in a state of calm order and she liked to watch things, including me, with her catlike eyes. Mr. Gray called her an attention-seeker and a troublemaker and as is the case with humans, these traits made her attractive, up to a point. She sought attention from her own kind, often desperately, though it wasn't the kind of attention you'd want. At the feeding trough I saw her lower her head to insert it between the bars, and then stick her neck out to one side so that her head was lying in the trough, under another cow's chin. Her neighbor couldn't feed. Ivy then turned her head and her eyes rolled up to look at her neighbor as the neighbor tried to find a way to feed: Hello. So it wasn't hard to understand why the other cows chased her away. Another day, with the herd gathered on one side of the barn, I noticed Ivy separating herself. She paced across to the far wall, then, using the length of the enclosure as a run-up, she ran herself head-first, full force, into the lower part of another cow's belly, which dented like a punched cushion. The cow moaned and moved away. Ivy retreated and took another run-up, targeting a different cow. She didn't show any fear. Perhaps she was brave, or she had no sense of consequence, of one thing leading to another, that events are linear and cannot simply be restated, and eventually, inexorably, a plausible story of cause-and-effect builds and breaks. She butted the bigger cows until they turned on her. Two matriarchs herded her to the back and crushed her against the stone wall. Ivy was obscured by their huge sides, each one a ton. Through their legs, as through a cage, I could see her thinner legs struggling and trembling. Then they released her and she buckled and dropped into the straw with her legs folded beneath her. She didn't get up for a while, her sides heaved. The bull had his head turned in another direction. Ivy was the only cow in the enclosure that he never mounted, even in play. She had no calf of her own. I knew what would have to happen to her if she was infertile. So I was hyperattentive to her interactions with the bull.

When the vet came we had to move the cows into a small enclosure. Mr. Gray opened the gate wide, offering freedom, but the herd, as though by prior agreement, backed away and gathered at the far end of the barn beside the wall. Then, from the back of the crowd, an interested face appeared. Ivy took one or two steps forward and the herd parted around her. The other cows turned from her and dipped their heads. Ivy seemed oblivious to their attention. She was interested only in what lay outside. She trotted forward, measured but steady, holding her nose in the air, nervous or optimistic. She ventured out into the yard, on the human side of the feeding trough. Her hooves made clopping sounds on the concrete floor. Only then did she turn back to her family. She made a grunting sound and the others urged one another forward and filtered through the gate. Mr. Gray called Ivy into the smaller enclosure and Ivy went willingly, silent and alert, her ears up. The others followed her there too.

I started walking alone at night around the village. Curtains were rarely closed, and the identical rectangular windows of the houses transformed the streets into rows of luminous pictures hanging on an indigo wall. Inside, more often than not, there were deeper layers of moving blue—the reflected light of the television made it look like everybody, forever, was watching documentaries about the ocean. An elderly woman brought a meal on a tray to a man sitting by the gas fire. A boy lay on his front on the carpet with his homework spread out in front of him. A teenager stood talking on a landline telephone, twisting the wire around his spare hand, looking out of the window. He was in the light and I was in the dark—he couldn't see me. There were no computers in these houses and no adults did work other than housework. No person was gazing into a handheld device. They were the final days of home life as it was then, discreet and private, with no aperture through which the social or the working life could pour. We didn't know it was the end of anything, of course. I am middle-aged now and still waiting for things to stop beginning. I used to walk around my urban neighborhood at dusk right up until I went into self-isolation. In winter especially, when darkness falls fast, there is a period of time at dusk before the blinds go down and it makes me like other people—all people—when I see them at home from the outside. I like them, even or perhaps especially when the domestic scene doesn't look cozy and happy. Now, from my desk, I can see right into the windows of the apartments opposite and these days I avert my eyes to stop myself from noticing what happens inside the homes. I'm here at all hours and I want to give my neighbors privacy—their own space is the only space they have these days. They can't get away from my gaze so I avert it. It's hard, especially with the woman who sits at her sewing machine right opposite me. The more I see her, the less she looks like Indira Gandhi. Maybe it's because she wears spectacles and knitted cardigans in rosy colors, not at all like Gandhi, or maybe it's because I have spent so much time sitting opposite her that I am seeing her for herself, but I don't want her to feel that I am watching her—I don't want any of my neighbors to feel that there is a detached witness to the spectacle of them fighting, or holding one another, or watching television.

When I was a child I rarely saw anything happen. I once saw the man who used to drive the digger shouting at his girlfriend with his face very close to hers. He looked distressed and she looked ultra-calm. That was during the time when the quarry was closed. And then there was the night in early spring. Raw, restless. Scraps of cloud seemed to glide swiftly right through the moon and between the stars and shaking, budding branches of the trees. I walked along the pavement past Grace's and Matthew's house; past June, who was still up, sitting alone under a bare lightbulb, knitting; past Clare's, where the lights were out; and up to the junction at the center of the village. The curtains were pulled across the bar room at the pub but light was coming through from behind them. Inside, something caught on one of the curtains and it pulled back for a second—a mass of bodies was visible and bright lights were echoed in mirrors and glasses, and pointed Christmas tree lights which were wound around the fixed spirit bottles. A beam of light fell out of the pub and stretched on the road, pointing toward me. The curtain dropped back again. When I looked away, into the hedge at the other side of the road, I could only see the imprint of the light in a cloud at the back of my eye. My night vision gradually returned.

A car appeared at the top of the lane. It jerked, slowed, and switched off its headlights. The engine cut out and the car rumbled down the slope. It wobbled like a newborn animal and gathered speed as it rolled toward the junction. It was small and white, greying yellow in the gloom, with dark patches of rust around the wheels. No light, no sound, floating in secret in the dark—a ghost car. I didn't recognize it.

The car took the corner at speed, then swerved sharply toward the pub, one tire mounting the pavement. I saw a fox in the middle of the road leap away in the other direction. She wrapped her tail around her flank and seemed to slip through her own body, then vanished into the hedge. The car corrected itself abruptly, dropping off the pavement onto the main road. It rolled past the pub and slowed along the street, as though it was about to stop, but then its lights picked up. The engine came on and I heard the gears ascend through the engine. Nobody inside the pub seemed to have noticed it. I hadn't seen the driver.

When we turned out the cows for the spring I noticed that Ivy went first and the others followed her. I remained inside the barn to drive out two calves, the first of that year, and I could hear the dry ground rumble as the herd gathered speed, running up the lane.

The calves had never been outside before and they were terrified. Both mothers had abandoned them in the rush and excitement of escape, and now one mother was braying out in the lane, the other too giddy to remember what she had left. The huge barn doors were open and pearly grey spring light flooded into the barn to reveal packed muck and straw that stopped at a foot-high cliff at the edge of the cattle enclosure. There was still a cold edge to the air. I could hear a cracking sound as the cows pulled the ends off the elder branches at the end of the lane. Mr. Gray climbed into the deep litter, packed so hard his boots were barely sinking, and tried to drive out the calves who, though tiny, were adamant. They streamed around him. He caught one of them and carried her like a baby, pinning her legs against his front, and staggered out into the lane and released her to her mother.

In his absence, the calf who remained behind relaxed. He moved around, sniffing the floor of his suddenly estranged home. There was a bantam sitting in a nest in a far corner and she was unsettled too—she chattered at the calf aggressively when he approached, and so he retreated. The mud was deep and dark and it had a grain, as wood does, the straws all falling in the same direction in patches, so that it appeared to be made up of brushstrokes. Looking closer, it was possible to see the thick straws of the bedding and, between them, dung. It was dung that held it all together, dung that comprised the negative space. Inside that, staring blankly into the straw I noticed an area of the soft mud twitch. An object, half buried in the debris and exposed by the disturbance, shone. I knelt beside it, feeling wet seeping through the cloth that covered my knees, and peered in. The object looked like a cocktail sausage which had been coated with orangey-brown garden fence varnish, but it was animated. Twitch. I brushed away the loose straw so I could see it. At one end it was twisted to a point like a fat metal screw. It twitched again and I drew back. It was something from a horror film. Something was trapped inside.

I looked up, as though the roof would give me the answer, and saw dusty corrugated plastic with spiderwebs around the beams. I looked back down at the throes of the entombed insect. It spasmed again and I almost could not bear to look at it any longer. I turned my head and got to my feet, brushed at the circles of brown wet on my knees. Then the object twitched differently, at either end, into a C-shape, and then it flipped, reversing the shape of the letter. I leaned down again to watch as it started to shake more violently, the way the roadside judders when a heavy vehicle hurtles through it at speed. It twisted back and forth and flipped itself, the contorted motion was sickening, like watching somebody being tortured. Then it was still. A minute passed. I waited. The object had given up. Calm descended.

Then one end of the plasticky shell cracked and two long dark thick hairs pushed out, lengthening and elongating. The shell smashed. Particles of brown dust showered around it. Another pair of hairs emerged and forced their way out, and then, by clawing over the edge of the shell, they hauled out the tiny, furry, dark face of a butterfly, emerging headfirst into the world, as babies do.

This creature was not like the red admirals which flopped around inside my house, out of season, drawn prematurely out of hibernation by the deceptive greenhouse warmth created through windows on a bright winter day. Sometimes my mother put out saucers of water for them, she had read somewhere that they died of thirst. This thing looked like a fat brown maggot with four feelers coming out of one end. The head and front legs forced their way out. Two more legs pushed through; more shell broke. The struggle did not become any easier. The creature's range of motion was limited to violently repetitive twitches. The legs batted against the sides of the shell, in futile labor with itself, until the nubby wings appeared, and a heavy abdomen was drawn out behind it, spunking tiny dots of pale brown liquid on the ground. The abandoned carapace was translucent, its pointed end intact, light radiating through its veined and ridged form like old stained glass. At last, it had become beautiful.

The creature was still crawling on the wet ground, dragging its huge abdomen behind it. I could see that it was an insect, an identity I had never quite recognized in butterflies before. I had always imagined that the butterfly popped out with ease. This change that I had seen looked painful. Things did not get easier after the moment of triumph. The hatched creature waddled soggily around in the dirt, its wings enlarging as I watched. I waited for an eruption of color which never came, though the reality had its own quieter glow. The wings, dark with damp, were brown, grey, pearl, olive, and chalk. From moment to moment, intense pink outlines appeared, in the fluff and on the wings, as the creature dried and continued to struggle toward the only form in which it had a small chance of survival. The calf was still stumbling around nearby. Its feet stabbed and sank into the ground with every step.

Mr. Gray reappeared. He chased the calf around the enclosure and the calf skipped past him, looking playful rather than desperate. Mr. Gray swore. The calf seemed determined to remain in this small and shitty place that was, for him, the world. When I looked back the moth had disappeared, trampled in or taken off.

I went outside and saw something I had not seen before. The bull's head was down, his nose almost touching the ground, and one front hoof was pawing the earth. He was facing Ivy. Mr. Gray swiftly pushed the calf into the field and pulled the metal gate toward us with a beckoning motion, so that I had to run backward as it scythed closed. Then we were on the other side and could only watch as the bull ran at Ivy. When he hit her she lifted slightly off the ground, then fell heavily and stayed down. The bull retreated and stood his ground again. Ivy didn't get up. The bull lowered his head and then, slowly, in a way that I found menacing, continued to lower it until his mouth reached the ground and he took a length of grass into his mouth, twitched his head slightly to uproot it. As he chewed, he moved around so that Ivy was no longer in his line of sight. I asked what Ivy had done and Mr. Gray shrugged.

In summer when the cows were out in the fields there was no need for me to feed them and so I didn't see Ivy again until she disappeared. Mr. Gray came knocking on our door, as he tended to when his cattle escaped. (He came to our house because my grandmother farmed nearby and there was, of necessity, a mutual dependency among local farmers in emergencies.) He told us that Ivy had escaped and she was stuck in the bog.

The wood in summer had an underwater light which felt morally improving, I could feel its good green grains under my skin. We heard Ivy before we saw her: a wet, mashing noise.

She had sunk beyond the tops of her legs into the black mud, and though in distress, she had composure. Her eyes rolled around to look at us, as though she was asking us what we planned to do now: our intelligence pitched against her physical weight in collaboration with the mud. The other cows were still in the field, beyond the fence.

Then something appeared at the top of the slope, so huge that the light dimmed. I knew, without looking, who it was, and I swiftly moved out of the way as the bull crashed down the slope, both heavier and more nimble than he appeared at rest. I did not know whether he was attempting to attack Ivy or to rescue her. He splashed right into the bog and was stopped by it a few feet away from her, higher than she was on the slope, and then he struggled. He was larger than Ivy, and because he kept moving he sank rapidly, centimeter by centimeter, before our eyes. I felt sorry for him when I saw how he flailed. I felt the weight he carried, as a living individual, struggling inside a body which constrained him to preside over the rest of the herd, and it had turned on him now. He was sinking toward a generic bovine state: meat. It was painful to watch this desperate negotiation between character, identity, and species take place inside his massive and flailing alpha male body. The bog dropped away at one edge, like an infinity pool, where the ground sloped down through the wood. I followed the line of the water as it ran down toward the river, and my eyes came to meet the abyss.

The drop was very small—only a few feet. The cold groundwater was perfectly clear when it escaped from the mud. It had carved a deep groove into a small rock, drip by drip, over centuries, millennia, or eons. Each drip slid to the edge of the rock's flat top and then hung on the edge of the surface for a long moment, pausing time altogether. Each drip was precisely the same size and shape, no bigger than a raindrop, and contained inside it an image of the wood turned upside down, barred with tiny trees whose leafy light spread like roots along the rounded base of the droplet. Then the drop dematerialized. It didn't seem to slide over the edge of the rock so much as simply evaporate, as though some thirsty force in the surrounding air gulped it up. Clearly, it was somehow dropping away, but though I followed its line I couldn't see where it went. The line where the water ran down had carved its way deep into the heart of the rock and at the center of this line there was a narrow margin that appeared, to my horrified wide eyes, pure depth. It was surrounded by the earth, mud, clear water, leaf mold, trees, rock, and then, right at the center, there was this infinitesimal abyss. Nothing, precisely drawn. A vacuum. Deep space.

The bull moaned again and recalled my attention. In his cow-handling voice, Mr. Gray told him to shut up. In his human voice, addressing me, he said that we would have to call the fire brigade and so we went back to the house to telephone, leaving the two animals where they were. I waited outside the house while he made the call. When he returned he said: "We'll take the car, I said I'd meet them in the turnout."

He gestured toward the car but I stopped dead before I reached it. It was the ghost car—the car I'd seen driving in silence past the pub. Mr. Gray noticed my surprise and he asked me what it was. I said that it was nothing and I got in.

THE FIRE ENGINE WAS IN the turnout when we arrived. There were two firemen, one man and one woman. The man shook Mr. Gray's hand and the woman stood back, one eyebrow raised, laughing without laughing. "We have to charge you Tommy," she said.

The woman had a clear, ringing voice. She talked in a different way from the way that most people spoke—directly and with rounded vowels, like a politician.

Mr. Gray asked what the fee was. The woman told him and he laughed. Then she said it again, more seriously, and that time he did not laugh.

They had equipment—a green tarpaulin which was rolled up, so heavy that it needed both of them to carry it. The woman handed Mr. Gray a flat board the size of a kitchen counter.

"I see you've got a helper," she said, looking at me. Mr. Gray explained that I was my grandmother's granddaughter, and useful with the cows. Then they looked at one another for a moment longer. The woman still had the merry look on her face, as though she was trying not to laugh, and I felt annoyed with them both. The woman went down on one knee and asked me politely whether I would be able to carry the straps. They were like long yellow safety belts with buckles at either end. Surreptitiously, as I walked behind the adults, I bit into one, and felt the points of my canines sink through the tight weave.

The cows were no deeper when we arrived at the spring. We spread out the tarpaulin to one side and the firewoman placed the board across the surface of the bog. Then the fireman swore and said that he had forgotten the shovels. While he returned to the fire engine, Mr. Gray and the woman debated which animal to dig out first. The woman wanted to get out the bull because he was heavier, and every centimeter he sank would add to the effort.

Mr. Gray disagreed. "If he gets out, she'll struggle"—he nodded at Ivy—"because she'll want to follow him. And she's already in deeper than he is."

His disagreement delighted the firewoman. Her eyes danced. "I'm sorry," she said. "Who is the professional here?"

The fireman came back with two spades and the adults took it in turn to dig around the bull. When they had dug four pits outside his legs, the fireman went to one side and the woman, on the other side of the bull, took the yellow belt and stretched out on her front, poking her arm down into the pit to feed the belt under the bull's belly to her colleague.

"This isn't what I pictured when I decided to be a firefighter," she said, but she didn't sound annoyed about it. She made me wonder what we were all doing there, how and why we had been channeled together to rescue two overfed bovines from the mud, only to have those cows killed later. One of us was paying to do this, the other adults were being paid, and yet other adults, far away, were weaving new yellow straps and riveting the buckles on. It all made sense, in terms of risk and reward, except for me—I was the only one who was there for the sake of being there. Just recently, when we first went into lockdown, I read a book in which an astrophysicist explained his job by saying: "Give us one huge and unlikely event—the Big Bang—and we can make everything else, rationally and mathematically, hang off that." In our situation, the Big Bang was Ivy's choice to go into the bog.

When the straps emerged through the hole we had dug on the other side the woman looped them at the muddy end so that the part we were holding was clean.

"Now it's a tug-of-war," she said.

We lined up along the straps, I was at the shoulder with Mr. Gray and the other two were at the hind legs. When we pulled I was surprised to feel the body lift smoothly, I had anticipated that the mud's embrace would be tighter. The bull allowed us to do what we were trying to do and when he was out he staggered to higher and firmer ground, where he allowed himself to be unstrapped, and then he lay down.

We took a break before beginning to work on Ivy. The fire-woman sat beside me on the tarpaulin and lit a cigarette. "I'm Cat," she said. She asked me if I wanted to try on her hat and I did, and so she took it off her head, revealing fluffy white-blond curls that made me think of chicks. When I had her hat on my head she made an approving sound and asked me what I wanted to be when I grew up. I told her that I was planning to be a ballerina and she took the hat back.

Ivy came up more easily. By the time she was out the bull was on his feet and tolerated Mr. Gray's patting his body to discern injury. There was nothing obviously wrong. Mr. Gray turned to Cat.

"Drink?" He made a glass-tipping motion with his hand.

Cat laughed humorlessly. "Hoping I'll settle your tab."

"I'll pay," said Mr. Gray curtly.

Cat moved her head indecisively from side to side. "I have to go back to the station and write up the story of this little escapade."

The mud in the bog was churned so badly that Mr. Gray had to fence it off, for the safety of humans on the footpath as well as to keep the cattle out. Several seasons later I could still see two black oval puddles where the cows had sunk in when, to my surprise, expensive new fences with walnut palings were put in place around an expanded area. When I spoke to Mr. Gray about it he said, articulating the words with ironic deference, that it was a site of *special* scientific interest. He explained that the churned mud and the fencing off had created the unusual conditions in which a rare species of curled-up worm could thrive. "The ecologist says that it is quite unique," he said, giving me a sly look from the side of his eyes. But I could hear that there was pride concealed in there too, the place meant something to him and he shared pleasure with the ecologist, as a new grandparent might share pleasure with the grandparent on the other side, no matter their personal differences.

When I saw Ivy again it was in late summer. She was standing very quietly, licking her side, in a small enclosure at the back of the farm buildings. I paused, resting my hands on the top bar of the gate, to stand with her for a moment. She had grown. She didn't turn to look at me.

I became aware of people walking along the public footpath which ran to my right. I turned and saw a Gurkha leaning over the other side of the corral. Retired members of the regiment had settled, or been settled, around the army camp on the other side of the local town, some bringing their families from Nepal. This man, wearing waterproof hiking clothing, was watching Ivy. He had a companion, an older woman, who was wearing a black dress with red and gold embroidery. The man said good morning to me and I said hello. The three of us turned back to look at Ivy, and in that moment, something twitched along the side of her body and in one long, smooth movement the shape of a tiny hoof and foreleg poked, perfectly formed in outline, through the other side of the stretched skin of her belly. Then it dropped away again and Ivy's body regained its smoothly curved surface. The image was hypernaturally precise, as clearly visible as something breaking the surface of water, and all three of us humans gave a short, automatic cry together. Our cries sounded almost identical—high-pitched, surprised, and pleased about it. We smiled at one another, embarrassed. Then the man said goodbye and the couple went on their walk, arms linked.

I went to bed early that night and when I woke up it was so dark and quiet that I knew it must be morning. I kneeled up to look out of my bedroom window. All the lights were out in the new houses. There were no foxes in the yard. It was one of those warm still nights during which the leaves on the trees appear to pick themselves up a little, like raised ears, flowers are swollen with shadow, the spaces between the petals turned into sponges for darkness, and the docks and tall weeds on the ground stand very straight, raised, and alert, long leaves like cupped hands, receiving and giving attention to the world beyond the confines of their own organism. A planet had risen, pale like a seed pearl above the hill. I lay back down in bed and was half asleep again when I heard an owl hunting in a nearby field with a lovely noise like hollow wood, and at the same time, coming from farther away, I heard the mail train trailing a long metal rhythm behind it. The two sounds combined as a rapture that exploded across the space and dispersed like a mushroom cloud through sighing leaves, hissing blades of grass, ringing inside exhaust pipes, making tiny vibrations inside the ears of deeply breathing, sleeping people, rolling out in the space inside the quarry. I wondered whether Ivy had calved. The sounds developed from, and then returned to, quiet.

In winter when the cows came in and I was there to feed them again, Ivy had changed. She was slower, steadier, and calmer. She stayed close to her son and she seemed satisfied, physically weighed down and not quite fit for purpose, like a person who has eaten too much and become sleepy. Ivy didn't butt into her neighbors or force a space around herself at the trough, and the other cows were at peace with her. I knew that this transformation was a natural process and could see that there was less violence and antagonism within the herd now. One day I noticed that Mr. Gray was watching her too, as she stood with glazed eyes, chewing. I couldn't help missing her, as though she had been consumed into the herd's larger identity. I realized that Ivy's character was more distinct to me than Mr. Gray's. In my mind, there was little about his character that distinguished him beyond the essential facts of his job.

In early autumn I saw an abandoned livestock truck with its back gates wide open, parked inside the yard outside the barn. I was waiting for the school bus on the opposite side of the road and I was early. I stood there and looked around me. The road was empty. I climbed up the ramp into the vehicle and stuck my own nose through the open slats in the green metal sides where the air streamed in. The quiet and emptiness included me. Then there was an eruption in a tree on the roadside—a sycamore. A crow took off like an explosion. In the aftermath, two dry leaves detached themselves from the tree. They drifted down and landed on the ground, each with the lightest trace of sound.

The muck from inside the cattle barn was left outside to rot in a heap, then it was spread on the large field to feed another season's hay. In winter the only mark of human presence that I could see inside this field was the deep tire tracks which ran from gate to gate along one side, tracing Mr. Gray's access route between the public road and his sheep pasture. I was walking along that track one day in early spring when something startled in front of me and spurted upward.

I halted and shaded my eyes, but the thing had vanished to reveal the sky's bare blue emptiness, heat wriggling above the horizon. At first quietly, then gradually rising in volume, I noticed a strange twirling sound, as though there was running water somewhere nearby. Eventually I placed its source: a bird, quite low, a little way in front of me. Black silky wings scrambling the air. The bird was larger than a thrush and smaller than a pigeon. It didn't try to get away from me. In fact, as it bobbed up and down, it seemed to be moving around me. If I stepped forward, it drew up and away from me. When I paused it dropped back down, pouring its loud song over me. It was trying to distract me. It was hiding something.

I scanned the slope. Early spring, I could see through the hedge. The new grass was coming up but it was still wintry—a sickly yellow color and inert after the heavy rainfall. The bird drew away from me and I decided that it was trying to pull me forward, a lure. It wanted me to follow it. I looked along the hedge, the track, and the slope for the thing. The bird looped and rose, wreathing its looping song around us both, as it hovered in front of me as the star must have hovered in front of the three kings, keeping an even distance. When I walked farther forward the bird intensified its effort, pushing its body upward in a straight line and then dropping. Its song rose in pitch and each bar of sound quickened and crashed into the next as a stream speeds up and tumbles over itself when it comes to a waterfall. The bird rolled, swooped, and cried, and then I spotted its nest. Her nest.

The eggs lay dumb together. They looked like chocolate eggs, the sugar-coated kind—green-grey with cocoa-colored speckles. The bird was close to me now. She was a weird creature, glossy black and white, wind streaming through a crest on her head. A lapwing. I saw hundreds of them on that field in the evenings when they collected together near the peak of the slope where the exposed grass didn't grow so tall. They looked like waterbirds, wading in a great flock, examining the spaces between their claws. This one, I noticed, was missing a small patch of feathers from her black bib.

I won't touch the eggs, I silently promised her as I moved toward the nest. I only want to see. I could sense her—a dark speck, a dark grain, a dark seed flowering into a shadow which covered me. As she bombed past my ear and shoulder I could hear her beak and wings slicing the air and I ducked. She banked and rose and fell on me again. I felt her cut my outline in the air. Her beak was sharp and the height and speed with which she fell gave her real weight—I felt, with a sense of surprise, that she was capable of hurting me, so I moved back, away from the nest, and looked at the eggs from a distance. There were four of them, laid in the wheel-rut. It was a neat fit but the tractor's treads were recently indented on the drying mud.

I went back again the next day and all four eggs had been smashed. There was no sign of the bird. Inside the nest the shells were crushed flat, their contents setting into a paste. I looked up—I was expecting that the mother would have stayed around— but she was nowhere to be seen, and I realized that my expectations were those of a human mother. A slight, sudden movement on the ground caught my eye, and I saw that there was another bird sitting a little way farther up the track. Another bird had laid another brood on the same track.

This mother was slower than the one the day before. She didn't take off when she saw me, she just sat there, looking at me. I could see her clearly. She looked intelligent and, to me, slightly comical, small bright eye glinting below her quiff, a professor in a party hat. Eventually, she heaved herself into the air, away from her eggs, and started to sing for me, which was what I was after. I made straight for the nest. Its eggs were darker brown than the four of the day before. They lay in brown earth. The mother had lined her bed with patties of the caked straw from the cattle barn which had been spread out on the field to feed the grass. That grass had journeyed from the field into the silage bale, through a cow's many stomachs, back up to the mouth and down again, through and out of the body into the deep litter of the winter barn, where it caked the wheat-straw bedding whose strata were trampled into a uniform sludge by their hooves. After the litter was removed from the barn it was rotted down in a pile, acquiring a hardened crust around its outer edge, and then in spring this shell was cracked open and the intensely rich inner substance was spread out to fertilize the field. This substance, still slowly melting into the roots of the grass, was what the lapwing carried in her own beak, fragment by fragment, to sit beneath her body, insulating her eggs, not far, no doubt, from that initial growth of grass which I saw as its origin, though in reality there was no origin and no end point. A place exports and circulates over distances, just as memory moves the past through the present and changes it. The matter that was in my presence then would continue to break down, build up, and move through places and bodies for a million billion trillion years, as far as I knew. The bird was rising and falling frantically. She had a small patch of feathers missing on her black bib: it was the same mother.

That evening I watched a music awards ceremony on television and saw a performance which went off-script and unraveled before my eyes. It began with a blue planet spinning in space on the screen at the back of the stadium. The planet looked small, hazy, and perfect. The music was one long low foreboding note. Slowly, a man's silhouette ascended against the earth, the dark blob of his head momentarily obscuring Nigeria, Benin, Togo, and Ghana, then Côte d'Ivoire, Liberia, and Sierra Leone, as he stepped higher and the earth turned on the screen behind him. The man came into view and I saw that it was Michael Jackson. As his face came into focus, the earth disappeared from the screen, leaving a circular hole through which I could see a bird's-eye view of a forest canopy from above, sunlit. Then a close-up of a lynx's intent eyes. Then a tree, falling in slow motion. Individual splinters swelled and pulled away from one another, the branches crashing together, then bouncing apart, like clapping hands.

When the drums came in, white smoke surged up from below Michael like sea spray, blowing his red and black clothing almost away from his body. Behind him a cloaked child appeared. She looked wan and lost, as though she had accidentally wandered out. She was followed by other children who filtered, apparently aimlessly, onstage, wearing dark clothing and rags, some singing, some weeping. The scene, as it developed, looked postapocalyptic and it made me feel strange—it was disturbing in a way that made me feel that I wanted to be disturbed. A man wearing white entered with a motionless baby in his arms, and he and a younger woman railed and wept over its body. A blond boy kneeled at the front of the stage, crying, praying, and singing. On the screen, the massive fluke of a humpback whale struck the ocean. Onstage, in the middle distance, Michael skipped with phenomenal grace and energy onto a small crane which looked not unlike the digger that was degrading above the quarry near my house.

As Michael rose above the audience and the music reached its peak, a white man ran out from the wings and positioned himself at the front of the stage. He didn't look out of place in the melee. I recognized him—he wasn't one of Michael's dancers, he was in another band. I experienced a sense of foreboding and sat up straighter. Tongues of fire exploded on the circular screen, so orange and bulbous that they appeared real, and I felt real heat in my face. Michael was high in the air singing above the stage when the young man dropped his trousers and wiggled his bum at the audience. The screen's flames turned to cooling towers belching dark grey smoke, then an emaciated baby weeping. The cameras focused on this screen as, in the blurred foreground, one of Michael's dancers chased away the interloper.

Then Michael landed back onstage and ascended the stairs toward the screen. His feet were as light as ever. His crowd parted and he descended through it with the beautiful, irregular assurance of a trickle of water running down a pane of glass. When he reached the precipice at the edge of the stage he seemed, for the first time, to be alone. He braced himself against a wind machine which was blowing a tempest into him so that his body, which was dancing against the force of it, appeared at the same time small and human, and touched with some fierce and transcendent force. He removed his black and red suit to reveal white clothing underneath. Then the music lightened as though a storm had passed over and the children gathered around Michael. They removed their ragged cloaks to reveal pinafores and school blazers in primary colors. Michael's face was exhausted but his body was still moving with the same light grace. People onstage approached him and then began to drift back to the wings. He hugged a woman wearing a printed dress and turban, clasping his hand around the back of her head with unfeigned fervor. He kissed the brow of a man wearing a skullcap and curls.

Then he addressed the room in his ethereal speaking voice. He told us how much rainforest burned every minute and how many children died of hunger in a year. He told us that he loved us and believed in all of us and then he walked, accompanied by the last of the children, into a tunnel of white light.

At school the next day everybody was talking about how Jarvis Cocker had jumped onstage and flashed during Michael Jackson's performance. Ann was upset—she said it was disgusting how Jarvis had ruined the message, which was bigger than all of us. Who would want to see Jarvis wiggling his bum when you could see Michael Jackson dance? People like him think they own the world, she said, and it was showing off. She sounded very much like Mrs. Hepton.

Ash said that he was happy to see Jarvis' arse. Michael, he said, needed taking down. "Do you even know how much money he has?"

Ann said that Michael had a gift and John Green said that there were rumors about him, did she not know them? Ann said that the rumors and the gift could both be true, which confounded the rest of us.

Jarvis Cocker, the man who had invaded the stage, was from a band whose biggest hit was "Common People." The band came from Sheffield, a city which was over an hour's drive away from my village, but which existed in northern England, within our world. It was a real place, the Colvins in the shop came from there. It wasn't Florida, or the Amazon, or Neverland. Around the playground, in the wake of the stage invasion, a story congealed. A millionaire's pretensions to saving the world were laughed at by a working-class northerner in a charity-shop suit, and it felt like justice. Nobody mentioned skin. Perhaps I did not see it or perhaps I didn't want to say. I returned to the lapwing field a week or two after that. Along the track there was a chain of three abandoned nests. The weather was warm, the cattle had been let out, and the gates between the fields opened. A heifer had wandered into the disused field and was bending over one of these nests licking up its mashed contents. Fragments of shell stuck to her tongue and a drool of dense, sticky yellow liquid connected her to the ground. I followed the line of perspective toward the crest of the slope, and there I saw a bird who was sitting on a new nest. As I walked toward her she rose, singing, elated by my return.

I passed two empty nests, the remains of four eggs lying in a neat cluster in each among the wreckage. A few feathers, a few muddy straws. The eggs which were laid on pale straw were pale in color and those laid on darker mud were dark brown. The eggs she made, inside her body, were formed in the colors of the ground she laid them onto. It was this, more than anything, that made me see that the bird was sensing things in ways I cannot reach. I didn't need to look for the bald patch on her white bib this time. I knew it was her.

The lapwing queered the way the land lay around her; the land rearranged me around it when I saw her smashed nests and connected them together to make a line. As I went about my life, most days, I believed that creatures did not communicate with one another across the boundary of the species. Humans exchanged language with other humans. Foxes marked territory so that other foxes knew where they were. The bull snorted only for his ladies. But when that lapwing sang on those two occasions I was certain that she was singing to me. She was trying to deceive me, using strange forms of communication within and beyond my own language, in defiance of what I thought of as sense. Her nest was reiterated, again and again, in almost the same place, and the effect in my mind, like the effect of repeating a single word over and over and over again, was of annihilating any possibility of meaning, and it gave me a feeling of meaninglessness that made me involuntarily laugh.

I have distance on it now. Looking out from inside my room, what she was doing doesn't feel as nihilistic or bewildering as I experienced it out in the field, when I was a child. Perhaps she felt each ruined nest as emptiness metastasizing. I know what it's like to keep on waiting for a baby who will never arrive. She kept on trying, as humans often do, until eventually she decided or accepted that being alone is inevitable and true. Then again, maybe she chose this place to nest not because she was too naive to know better but because her priorities didn't occur to me, or perhaps she didn't have priorities, perhaps there was nothing except the desire to make a good nest and lay and lay and lay and lay and lay and lay and lay. I had not known the two lines of mud, indented on the edge of the field, as anything other than a track for vehicles. I had not seen the track as something perfectly shaped for a feathered body to sit, seeing in all directions, that the deepenings where the tractor sank into softer mud were not only ruts but also cradles. For the tractor driver, as for most people, this wasn't because he hated the lapwing but because he hadn't known that she was in his space, or that he was in hers. From this distance, it's clear to me that the two things converged in the same landscape, the white man on television assuming his right to the stage and the farmer taking the road. Neither of them intended to cause harm. That's what's scary.

From isolation, I can see micro-colonies everywhere. I'm ruthless in my battle with the clothes moths over particular territories, even though the battle is life or death to them and I could live without my white sweatshirt. On the windowsills and guttering of the roofs visible from my window I can see the spikes which state that the human right to a clean surface has precedence over a bird's right to land. In the park at the end of my road there are metal dividers on the bench that assert the priority of a wealthy person's desire to sit down over a homeless person's need to sleep. In isolation, as an adult, I can see what Ann was trying to articulate, as a child in the middle of it all—how white culture loves to tell itself, in its stories, its science, its architecture, its landscaping, that it needs to be selfish to be at its best. But there is only one Earth Song and it is a weird and messy song of abusers who are also victims, ignorant schoolchildren, bewildered adults, money, common people, a humpback whale, an emaciated baby, a bird's egg, music executives, domineering fathers, a lynx's intent eyes, a genius, a bacterium, and a forest on fire.

A track ran down from the lapwing field and around the back of Mr. Gray's farm, ending at a stile onto the main street. There was one shop, a post office, which was run by Mrs. and Mr. Colvin. It was impossible to dislike Mr. Colvin: he was cheery and welcoming, and there was a deep sadness that lingered around him. When he stood up to fetch sweets from the rack behind the counter his stance was primate-like, round-shouldered with drooping arms. In the human body this is a posture of defeat, and yet, each time I went into the shop he would rise up out of his chair and greet me with pleasure, as though I had come to visit him, personally, and he was delighted that I had bothered. Mrs. Colvin greeted the customers very differently and always with the same phrase: "What are you after, then?" Mrs. Colvin looked older than her husband, though they both looked after themselves, neat clothing and a clean shop. A mop, propped up in the front corner, had been known to follow muddy customers when they walked on the tiled floor. Mrs. Colvin communicated a mistrust of her customers, especially children, with the deployment of this prosthetic, and her eyes followed me vigilantly below an immovable frown as I looked along the shelves. Because she made me feel untrustworthy, I acted shiftily in her presence, glancing over my shoulder to follow her eyes following me, but even so, shamelessly, I always went right to the back of her shop to browse a set of shelves from which I never bought anything: two racks, one which had sewing scissors and thread on it, the other with tinned meat. Behind them, an open door with a curtain of brightly colored ribbons hanging over it gave a view of the Colvins' sofa and television, and out to their kitchen at the back. The shop was the street-facing room of their home. The view into the back of the building was ordinary but forbidden and I always tried to catch a glimpse through the ribbons, which drifted and fell as I felt Mrs. Colvin's eyes on my back.

Inevitably, as people went in to pick up milk or child allowance, there were shared stories about exchanges that had been witnessed between Mr. and Mrs. Jokes were made, why did he put up with her, etc. Mr. Colvin's seat was positioned in the frame of the large shop window. I remembered him in my adult life when I went to a zoo in Germany, where I spent some time watching a chimpanzee who was sitting straight-backed on an artificial rock, eating a pear whose pale flesh was browning, and gazing meditatively into open air, somewhere above the heads of the wall of human beings that was jostling and pointing its phones a few meters away. The ape's poise and self-containment, pretending that they were not an object of interest, impressed me. The Colvins didn't have children. She, in particular, was seen as a threat.

Ann and I made hoax calls from the telephone box opposite the shop. The first time, we recited obscenities in long strings into the receiver, holding the mouthpiece between us. But we couldn't hear what the operator was saying, with the receiver like that, and we wanted to experience the response. We decided to invent an emergency.

I spoke first. The operator, a woman, asked for details of the car accident and I gave her details, the smell of melted rubber, blood soaking through hair, until I had convinced myself. The operator told me to calm down and I ended the call.

Then Ann tried a fire. She was composed for longer, following my responses along the path of the script that the first operator had used on me.

Half an hour later a fire engine stopped outside the pub. Ann and I watched in silence from the window of the bedroom that she shared with her sisters. We clasped our hands together and didn't speak. We didn't need to, the sense of power and fulfillment was so strong. Uniformed adults milled around and talked to the landlord, went in and out of the pub. They didn't do anything, nor did they leave. We went downstairs to watch TV before they left.

After this success we intensified our work. The shop front faced the telephone box but Mr. and Mrs. Colvin never came out. One day when the shop was closed I happened to glance upward through the panes of glass inside the telephone box and I saw a figure in the upstairs window of the shop, which was closed. She was like a ghost, standing in front of the white gauze curtain looking down on us with her sharp eyes. Shop-smart. Pale yellow turtleneck and a sweep of brushed hair.

The second time we succeeded in provoking a response, it was one lone police car and it drove right up to the phone booth. Ann and I were sitting on the bench below the war memorial, a little way along the road, almost out of sight. An officer climbed out of the car and looked around. When she saw that there was nobody in or near the telephone booth, she crossed the road and went into the village shop. A few minutes later she came out again and drove away.

After that nothing happened for a while. Ann and I continued to call but we didn't succeed in summoning anybody. We wanted to get an ambulance out, to complete the set. Sometimes when we were inside the phone booth, I looked up and Mrs. Colvin would be there, watching us from her bedroom window with her hooded expression. Then, another day when the shop was closed, Ann and I were in the phone booth together, and through the narrow window-pane, I caught sight of Mrs. Colvin across the road. She had appeared in her slippers at the front of her closed shop, at the place on the concrete where the fruit and vegetable rack stood on weekdays. She must have come around the side of the house. She beckoned to me.

I obeyed, helplessly, and Ann trailed behind me. I couldn't take my eyes off the Colvin slippers—pink, moccasin-style, with sheep's wool clouding around her bare ankles. The ankles had a faintly grey appearance.

"You'll need to stop that now," said Mrs. Colvin.

"Why?" asked Ann.

"Because they'll catch you."

"We're not doing anything to catch," I said quickly.

"They want me to tell them who it is," Mrs. Colvin replied.

We all stood and we all looked at one another. She gave us time. I hadn't realized how placeable we were. Nobody was interested in tracing me. No person was keeping tabs on all the emergencies in the entire country as they flowed through the call center, which I'd never imagined as something located in a real place, with walls and a ceiling.

"I told them," said Mrs. Colvin, "that I haven't seen anything."

For a second, then, I thought she was about to laugh. The corners of her mouth lifted and her face took on a look of deep mischief. But the habitual frown lowered itself down over her features again. She turned and walked back into the house, the backs of her slippers patting the concrete. She never told anybody—not the police, or school, or parents. We stopped making calls.

Early in the morning on the days when the shop was open, on the spot where Mrs. Colvin had stood, the fresh food rack was carried out front by her husband and placed to face the road. He carried it back in again at dusk. The produce it offered was local—though local produce was not any kind of boast: soft onions, wrinkled potatoes, leeks containing concentric layers of grit—with the exception of the mottled brown and yellow bananas that hung on meat hooks from the old newspaper rack. Each one was decorated with a bright blue sticker on which there was a lady in a frothy dress wearing a basket of fruit on her head who looked phenomenally happy. The bananas were different to all other fruit and Ann, who was diabetic, wasn't allowed to eat them, which made them more delicious to both of us. They cost less than sweets and came in a brown paper bag which became a pouch full of their strange sweet scent. One day, at home, my mother's basket was lying open on the table. The basket was the one she used when she walked to the shop. It was made out of old straw with a brown leather strip around the top, and only had a handle on one side. I didn't like it because the straw was frayed and stabbed the skin on my wrist. Inside it that day I could see that there was a paper bag whose shape outlined the crescent curves of its contents.

I picked up this bag and untwisted its corners, took out a banana, peeled, and bit. I was still looking at the open mouth of the paper bag when a spider jumped out. It sprang onto the table, all eight legs landing at the same time, and then it stood still. I did not take my eyes away. The spider was elegant—long-legged, with a body tapered like a teardrop and covered in a fine grey fuzz like the mold that forms on old food. The banana was ripe. It had that strange and delicious poison taste that also slants through pear drops, solvents, and aerosols. The chemical taste spiked my airways as the banana mushed in my mouth. I placed a glass over the spider and went to find a parent.

When I came back with my mother the spider was dashing madly halfway up the glass, then somersaulting to land on its feet. We examined the mottled bananas and inspected the inside of the paper bag. We could find no trace of an egg sac. My mother said that the spider was probably harmless and that it was interesting. She took it out and dropped it in the yard. It landed on its feet again, then froze for a second on the concrete, and then it dashed so quickly that my eyes interpreted a single grey line between its body, which my mind believed was still in that same place on the concrete, and the rough patch below the trees, into which it had disappeared.

It was unlikely that the spider was venomous. It was unlikely that it would survive in the cold north. It was almost impossible that it would have been able to breed. Still. Its presence haunted that patch of the garden. For years, I always wore shoes there. The corners of my eyes caught grey shadows and in the mornings I started to notice something I had never noticed before: thin, see-through silk threads which stretched through the air across the back door. They seemed to be floating—there was no visible beginning or end—I couldn't see what they were attached to. Eventually this unnatural hyper-awareness faded. I had forgotten the spider by my early twenties, when it suddenly rose back out of my memory one summer. I had received a grant from university to visit an octogenarian poet who lived in rural Nicaragua, and was traveling with my boyfriend on buses overland from San Jose until, several days into the journey, my boyfriend fell ill. He curled awkwardly in his reclining seat, twisting with cramps, muttering short broken stories and laughing in a creepy way. At the next stop we left the bus and went to the near-est hospital where he was diagnosed with dengue fever and put on a drip. The other beds in the ward were occupied by quiet, grey-haired people screened from one another with white mosquito nets, like sleeping beauties. At one end of the ward there was a square space let into the wall, looking out onto a courtyard in which there were two slender swaying trees. The serious doctor looked very young. "Your boyfriend could hemorrhage and die in a matter of hours," she told me.

I found a room in a hostel in the nearest village. The hostel was run by a Nicaraguan woman and her American husband and was largely empty, though every night a few American surfers arrived late and stayed over on the long-distance drive from California to Costa Rica. One evening, one of these men followed me back to my room when I was leaving the shower block. He was drunk and it was easy to get away from him, but after that I showered in the morn-ing and started carrying my keys in my fist with the pointed end between my fingers when I cycled out to the hospital along the long, straight, deserted road, all along which, on both sides, in regimented rows, as far as the eye could see, banana trees were growing.

I had never seen a banana on a tree before and it looked strange to me because the fruit grew inside large blue plastic bags. The bags were suspended around each developing bunch—protecting them, I suppose, from living things. Wires were strung between the trees as though holding the grove together, each line leading toward some concealed center. The plantation road was local, with little traffic. It wasn't used on the international routes along which the Americans drove and its surface was not tarmac but compacted chalky stone. My rented bicycle was large and sturdy—I wouldn't have been able to lift it onto a bus—with wide tires that coped well with their circumstances.

I cycled out to the hospital every day and sat in the light-filled ward, talking or reading to my boyfriend, or sometimes just sitting quietly at the end of his bed in the path of the cool breeze that streamed between the windows. My boyfriend introduced me to the older men and women in the beds around him. Sometimes I would bring a thriller from the hostel bookshelf, or American food from the vending machine. I felt peaceful in the ward, until the serious doctor appeared to give me the daily update on his recovery. She instructed me to bring grape juice, which would help my boyfriend's body to replenish its platelets. The doctor was the only person who induced in me a sense of conscience about our presence in that place, moving around with the rich person's entitlement and the young person's sense of invulnerability, without knowing how to inhabit the world safely, and then expecting her to clean up our mess, which she did. My boyfriend had become extremely thin. His limp, emaciated forearm, lying along the starched blanket, made me think of the pictures of people who were in their final days of life with AIDS and when I talked to him, I hoped that he couldn't see, through the mosquito net, that I had lifted my eyes to the window to avoid looking at him because it was painful for me to do so, and I rightly felt ashamed of myself. We had been careless in traveling to Nicaragua, careless in falling ill, careless about the scrunched US dollars that we used to settle the hospital bill. The glucose drip was more expensive than the doctor's care. Then one day she said that my boyfriend's red blood cell count was climbing and he could be discharged in a few days.

The day before he was due to leave I cycled along the road through the banana plantation with Pringles and grape juice in my basket. Plastic bags hung motionless on the banana trees, not crinkling and cracking as they sometimes did. There was no wind at all. I heard, at first dimly, and then growing closer, the clank of another bicycle chain. The clanks came more frequently as the bicycle sped up and they grew louder as it got closer. I had been told about the power of suggestion. I maintained an even speed, an even grip on the keys between my fingers. I did not look over my shoulder.

As the bicycle drew level with mine I tried to recall the feeling I'd had as a child on what I thought of as my own territory, when I'd cycled all day alone wherever I wanted, and if a strange man had approached me I wouldn't have felt threatened with violence, I would have felt threatened with boredom. It *was* a man behind me, slight, perhaps in his fifties, his hair not yet greying beneath a conical straw hat. He smiled. We greeted one another and then, as though by agreement, we both slowed and dismounted so that we could walk alongside one another, wheeling our bicycles. I kept the key in my hand.

For a while we did not say anything. Then the man pointed to the trees. He said something which sounded to me like "agriculture," and he paused so that he could mime eating a banana. This made me laugh, because eating a banana is one of the things that can be mimed, like cleaning a window or being trapped inside a box. The man laughed with me. I pointed to the man and said the word which sounded like agriculture again, as a question, and he nodded, and drew with his finger in the air a periodically dipping line from tree to tree. I nodded, pointed to myself, and said, "Farmer," "Cows," in French. Then I said "No," shook my head, pointed at the very center of my chest, and said "Student," in English.

The man nodded. We wheeled along, his bicycle squeaking at each turn of the wheel. He removed his conical straw hat and pointed at it. "*China,*" he said. "*Mucha gente.*"

I shook my head.

"*Mucha gente,*" he said, again. "*Poco tierra.*"

I laughed uneasily and wondered where he was going with this, but he wasn't going anywhere, or if he was I couldn't follow him there—I nodded and said "Aah" and he laughed. With effort, erratically, we communicated information to one another—I told him about my boyfriend's dengue fever and he told me about his children—but the conversation was at its best when we were laughing and it was only funny when it failed. When I reached the hospital the man mounted his bicycle again and went on.

After my boyfriend was discharged from the hospital we gave up our plan to reach the octogenarian poet in his remote location. Instead we took overnight buses through Costa Rica to an island off the coast of Panama, where we spent the remains of our summer drinking beer in beach bars and learning to surf. With retrospect, our change of course was inevitable. It felt natural.

In Panama each morning we purchased avocados and bananas from a stall, paying with American dollars. The bananas had a familiar blue sticker on: it was the same Chiquita I had known during my childhood. She hadn't aged. The overloaded basket of fruit was still balanced, precariously, on her head. It seemed strange that the bananas on the stall in Panama were the same brand as those which browned on the rack in the village shop, and yet the supply chain had always been in plain sight, link for link. In the village, through my childhood, trucks blasted along the road and the trucks which took stone out of the quarry dropped over the horizon at the motorway, like characters in a computer game who drop over the edge of the created dimensions. I saw the banana woman again, somewhere else, recently. Last year a stack of shipping containers was moved onto an area of wasteland near the center of the city near my house. Signs went up outside: Container Park. Local Roastery, Micro-brewery, Artisan Bakery. The containers bore their original markings—Maersk, "K" Line, Hanjin, and Chiquita, which had a picture of a bunch of unblemished bananas on its rippled metal side. Inside it was a coffee shop.

When I first saw that container I thought about the man I'd met inside the banana plantation, years earlier, but I couldn't remember his face. Since then I had read about Nicaraguan banana workers who had brought a court case against Dole for the use of a nematicide, during the 1980s and 1990s, which had made many men sterile. The man I met was of this generation. I'd felt scared when I was cycling through the banana trees. I had felt that my body was vulnerable to its strange environment. In fact it was the other way round. And yet, somewhere in the distance his full being had vanished, reduced by perspective, and I could see how the same features of perspective applied to me: from another point in the supply chain my whole life would appear as a link. A few pounds or dollars a year, an open hand and an empty mouth.

I was the only customer inside the shipping container. The young man behind the counter was not especially welcoming and he was slow to ask me what I wanted, slower to make the coffee, but his lack of enthusiasm made me feel relaxed. A boy with tangled blond hair was sitting on a box beside him, playing on a device. The man caught my eye and gave a lopsided smile. "Half-term."

I took my coffee to the other end of the container. It was so expensive and so delicious that it was mildly physically painful to drink it. I looked up to the low ceilings and felt other freight pressing in around me, inside the container, inside this strange engineered adult playground, the pop-up container park. Phantom bales of wires, electronics, cardboard boxes, cramped human beings in hiding, crates of fruit long off-loaded. Energy passes through the shipping container, the falling raindrop, the starchy sugar, the contrail, the human body. This was the banana spider's web, it was greater than all of us in that it had been alive and present at every connection, the plantation, factory, freight container, shop, kitchen table. It was still out there, beyond my mind's holding capacity, spinning out contacts between a child with a splintered straw bag and a man in a frayed straw hat, smooth skinned, too laid-back to oil his bicycle chain, frustrated with his younger daughter, making time to talk to a passing stranger to whom he was attached not by love, family, or shared interests, not even by experience, place, or

DAISY HILDYARD   ▪   133

culture, but by infrastructure. I never saw the spider again but it had presence nonetheless—it haunted me. One day I asked my mother why I didn't have an accent. The Queen has an accent, I explained, and Ms. Carr, like all Scottish people, has an accent. But my own voice does not have any accent. I am normal.

My mother gently explained to me that we had not, as a family, traveled. It was only natural that I would believe that my small world was the whole world. There were many other worlds, she told me, and none of them were central. It was impossible to have a voice which didn't have an accent. I found this hard to believe. In the gardens around my home there were flowers from all over the world, many of which, by flagging, made it clear that they did not want to live there. Other plants were so well fitted that they were reproducing beyond control—in my own garden there were raspberry canes that had gone feral along the stretch of bare verge where there were no houses across the road, on the outer stretch of the main street running toward the shop. Every year we had to remove the prickly stems of the baby plants which were advancing across our lawn toward Matthew's. Out on the roadside the raspberries grew along the verges, inedible because the road became gritty with quarry dust in early summer and any vehicle would make this dust part, then roll in clouds toward the sides, so that each verge-side berry was coated in a pale plaster. The berries were small and soft. You couldn't rinse the dust away without them pulping between your hands, red juice running down the drain, leaving a cluster of seeds like grit between the fingers. Even today, I don't know how commercial raspberry growers manage to keep the berries so separate and individual when the plant has a deep desire for its every berry to merge. The membranes surrounding each swollen juice-pouch are painfully thin. People say that growing plants is a calming thing to do but in my experience it is more often enraging: no matter how tenderly I cradle the box of raspberries on the way home from the allotment, by the time they arrive in the kitchen they have gathered together in an indeterminate mush, often containing small, uncategorizable creatures. It tastes the same, I tell myself, but it doesn't taste anything like the beautiful, flavorless chiller-cabinet individuals who dwell in boxes with rounded corners, a clean window of film, and an oblong of absorbent material that is thoughtfully placed as a mat on which the berries can rest, each one with its separate identity intact. I gave up my allotment early this year. It seemed wise to keep out of public places, or anywhere with live airborne matter. Instead, I have a window box crowded with coral-colored geraniums that I adore.

Yesterday I was woken up in the early hours by my smoke alarm. I thought it was doubly inert—the battery was dead, and I'd disconnected it—but apparently not, at 3 A.M. it began to pip. The light when I switched it on was blinding. I stood on a chair, squinting into the fixture. Luckily the "Test & Hush" button worked and a beautiful silence fell over everything like a veil of night sky. I turned off the light again and went to fetch a glass of water. As I drank, I remembered my window box. I hadn't watered it for a while and I always watered at night, in the cool, when the roots hold more water. My glass was still half full and so I opened the window and poured the rest over the parched earth. It had been a hot day. I pressed my fingertips into the soil and it was still warm. It smelled good.

One window was illuminated opposite me. The woman sat at her sewing machine. She was wearing her glasses and a fluffy pale pink dressing gown. I could hear the machine whirring. When the woman lifted out her work the sound died away. In that moment, I closed my window and it gave a clunk that rang out across the quiet neighborhood. The woman looked up, directly at me. We were the only two people awake in the world and I thought for a moment that we would wave, but she looked quickly down at her work again as though she was too busy to lift her hand and too absorbed in her work to notice me standing opposite her. Very English, I thought, whatever. The water made a buzzing sound as it trickled down, in its own time, through the roots and the dry loose soil.

In my childhood garden the raspberry plants moved forward as an army, each stalk very straight and upright, marching from one post to the next. The smallest and weakest new canes were on the front line, shorter than those behind them as they moved into unknown territory. The tiny plants I uprooted had four leaves on their heads, and the prickles on their stalks were still so tender that they bent under pressure from finger and thumb. The roots did not go down deep, and yet, often, when I pulled out a stem, it would only shoot up again in the same place a few weeks later. They were secure underground, where they could move around obstacles and creep below turf and fences, but once they pushed up into the air they had to force the close-knit grass roots to make space for an uprising shoot, and there was always a point at which their topmost leaves would announce them above the grass. This was the place of danger, where they became visible to the weeders.

As the raspberries spread outside the garden the weeds—thistles, cow parsley, dandelion, docks—flew in from the roadside. Their free movement exposed the weakness of the human community's property boundaries. Kale and oilseed rape escaped organized existence in the crop fields and grew in splurges along the sides of the road, where they were cut back in summer by the council together with the long grasses and ropes of purple bramble: the plants which escaped the lawn edging tool were those which grew into and through the wire fences, and the seeds, spores, droplets, and molecules infiltrating the structure of a fence or even, some of them, passing through the open pores of a red brick, never participated in the collective consent to believe in those boundaries. In another part of the space, to the airplanes and meteors that passed overhead, our little fences were nothing. Up in the air, above my head, there were wires which led to the telephone box opposite the village shop where the telegraph cables radiated from a central pole. The wires were placed regularly and ran in all directions like the markings on a clock, criss-crossing between buildings and encircling the village with a long dipping line along the outer road past my house and around the back, opposite the house in which Alice used to live. She was gone.

When I walked past, soon after the curtains were taken down, I could see that most of her furniture was still in the kitchen. The ash tree was standing beside the gateway and something was happening at a node, low down on the rotten trunk. A long, slender grey branch was extending itself, pushing out black buds and, at the end, a flourish of trembling green leaves. The rest of the tree was still rotting—the living branch rose out of the black sodden wood and pointed into the air like a hand poking through grave turf.

The branch was growing above the place where Alice had hacked a mouth-shaped notch into the trunk, as though the anger and the space that she had knocked into the wood had revived it. Alice had been moved out by her son. He said she could no longer look after herself. He had planning permission to turn her home into holiday flats for walkers. I walked on, away from the house, and encountered Nic, Clare's mother, walking in the other direction. We stopped and said hello. Nic was wearing a peach-colored sweater with a small, brown-red stain which had spread into a flower shape. I must have been staring because she touched it. "Adam had a nosebleed."

I nodded. "He does that at school," I said. He was often sent to the back of the classroom to stand over the sink with a stack of green paper towels pressed to his face.

Nic raised her eyebrows. "Not on your sweater, I hope."

I wanted to ask after Clare but I didn't know what it was that I needed to ask. There was a fuzzy noise above us and I looked up to see hundreds of starlings on the wires, some stable on a thick twisted metal cable, others perched along another, slightly lower, thin and rubber-coated line—like a clothesline. The birds who were perched on this line were tipping back and forward like mechanical toys, trying to establish balance. The motions flowed back and forth along the wires. The birds' tales fanned out against the bright sky, claws circling the wire, each feather straining against the pull. I saw a space open up on the larger metal cable—one bird abandoned its perch and dropped down into the hedge. All at once, several birds from the thin wire converged on the vacated space. Priority was quickly and invisibly established: one bird settled into the new position and the others returned to the wobbly wire without a fight.

"Is it migration?" I asked. I knew that the birds gathered together on the wires before they went.

Nic snorted. "At this time of year? Anyway those ones don't go anywhere."

I shrugged. "Okay, then."

I started to walk on, but Nic called after me. "Do you want to ask about Clare?"

I nodded and I said the thing that I thought she wanted me to say.

"She's a lot better," said Nic.

I nodded again. I already knew that, I'd seen Clare in the garden when I walked past on my way back from the school bus. She was still very thin but she was up. Her hair had grown back and she'd kept it short. She looked like a wicked elf.

"Will she be at school then?"

"She won't go back to junior school," said Nic. "She'll start at secondary."

I felt angry when Nic said that—I had been waiting for Clare's return. It was difficult to see her as a victim, she was the one who called the shots. She had got herself out of many days, terms, years, and endless afternoon hours of school.

Nic asked about my parents and I said that they were the same as usual. I asked about Dmitri and Nic said, "He's on the rig."

"What?"

"He left the quarry. They haven't been digging since last summer."

I stared at her. "What's a rig?"

"A factory on the sea where they drill for oil."

There was a pause. I was still staring. "Does he like it?"

Nic shrugged. "Every day's the same, but he only works twenty weeks in the year."

After we parted I walked over to the quarry to sit on the new wall. Things had changed there too. Large dirty white bags full of sandy gravel were piled up in the base. Over months, more bags were added to it and it became a wall. The wall became a high bank, and then production de-escalated and no more were added.

The bank had a stadium structure, each layer of bags stepped back from the lower layer. When I climbed on it with Ann, the bags at the top were soft and internally mobile like beanbags, but those at the bottom were soaked by rain and settled into a rough concrete substance. Down there, giant fungi whose pale fruiting bodies, the size, color, and shape of half a birthday cake, were thriving. At dawn and twilight small groups of deer made their way down from the wood's edge to eat them. I knew this because two men I didn't recognize turned up one weekend morning and sat on plastic chairs, long rifles leaning against the sides, waiting to shoot them, though from what I could see the men were more interested in smoking rollies, drinking from the shared hip flask, and chatting to one another than they were in killing animals. It looked peaceful enough. Either the deer were wise to it or the men found a better place—they only came for a few weeks and then they stopped, leaving behind a few holes in the bags of gravel in the places where they had missed potshots at rabbits. Around these holes the bags began to sag and fray, and perhaps the mammals nibbled and scratched them. Weeds and more fungi spread into the gaps and spaces.

Soon after that, when I was sitting up at the top of that bank with Ann, I asked her if she knew what had happened with the quarry.

"Of course I do," she said irritably. "What, do you walk around with your eyes closed?"

"Tell me."

Ann sighed. "The Chinese city's finished. Or anyway they don't need our gravel anymore, maybe they've got their own. Nobody's buying."

I pictured a brand-new city built entirely out of rubble. Sky-scrapers with many crumbly flats in them and inside one, I could see the digger driver, shouting at his girlfriend. Ann was kicking her legs against the hard sides of the bags and I looked down. The bags at the base, I noticed, had been split neatly with a sharp implement, each one with a straight cut down its side so that the contents were bleeding out onto the ground. I pointed this out to Ann.

"They take the stones out of the ground and then they just put them back in again," she said wearily, and she sighed again.

It was the weekend before the beginning of the summer holidays, I didn't know why she was being so moody. "What's your problem?"

Ann continued to bounce her heels off the sides of the bag, faster and faster, until I elbowed her. "I hate the holidays."

Sometimes, rarely, she talked about her father who lived in a caravan. I knew that she looked forward to staying there and was then disappointed when she went. Her father went out to work for long hours and Ann had to make cold food for her sisters.

"At school," she said, "there's a point. You're going somewhere."

I could feel damp seeping through the bags and into the back of my jeans. "Where do you want to go?"

She shook her head. "I get a sick feeling when there's nothing to do all day. I can hear a horrible voice saying *I can't* going around inside my head." We sat quietly for a while. "At school you all come to my table when you don't know the answer."

She looked at me without turning her head. I saw her sidelong, her eyes flicking toward me behind her glasses. She didn't say anything else.

On the last day of term there was a school fair—stalls, races, and, that year only, there was a hot-air balloon in the nearby field. It was attached to the ground with a long thick rope. You could ride up, then down again, for 50p.

The balloon was owned by a small person with short fair hair and a wrinkled face. A stepladder stood at the side of the basket, which was woven and had worn brown leather padding around the edge. As I climbed up the stepladder and dropped in I had a weird feeling that I was inside my mother's frayed shopping basket—like a grocery.

I paid my money. The basket filled up until there were ten of us in there.

Mrs. Hepton joined at the last minute. Ms. Carr, who was heavily pregnant again, stood at the side to watch.

The small person stood on a crate to reach the flame below the balloon. We bumped off the ground and Mrs. Hepton groaned. "I'm not sure if I'm going to like this."

A boy pushed his toes into the side of the basket and leaned right out. The balloonist shouted at him to stand down. Mrs. Hepton told him to sit on the floor, where he wouldn't be able to see the view. He obeyed her.

I found a space at the edge so that I could look down. As we moved upward I could see farther. The school and its village reduced in size and I could see more and more landscape until I could see how it connected to my own village. I could see the quarry, the fields, roads, the big house, the hill where we went mushrooming, and the river. I couldn't see detail. Anything small could go missing from this view and the view wouldn't change.

We had reached the end of the rope. The balloonist pulled a lever which sent a flame into the balloon, and then climbed down from the crate and came to stand beside me.

I asked: "Will we go into space?"

The person replied seriously. "Even if the rope breaks, we wouldn't be able to leave the atmosphere."

Mrs. Hepton had turned away from the side and covered her eyes. "I can't look."

The boy on the floor was tapping a rhythm on my ankle with his toe. I knew that we were stable, held by the rope, floating at a level height. When I looked down I could see tiny blue curtains, half drawn in a bedroom window, and a bulb of midges lit up in the air between two trees. When I lifted my eyes I could see space.

WHEN I WAS CONSIDERED OLD enough to work with sharp implements I was sitting in the classroom one day with a scalpel in one hand and a magnifying glass in the other, watching something moving under my lens. I used the scalpel to part the dark material until I reached it—a fine neon-green curved line, humped in the middle. It looked like a caterpillar but it was as fine as a hair. I put up my hand, the teacher didn't see me. He was new—Ms. Carr's maternity replacement—and I couldn't remember his name. I waited, but he was facing the other way, squatting beside Lyona's desk to remonstrate with her in a low voice. Several girls had refused to touch the owl pellets. They said that it was shit. The teacher said that it was in fact not shit. My arm began to ache. I put my hand down and picked up the magnifying glass again.

The magnifying glass exploded everything in view. When I held it over the pellet, I could see the baby caterpillar climbing up the dead material as though it was a mountain. Then its front end disappeared inside and I realized that the caterpillar was feeding; death was only recycling. The creature who had made that fur and skin, already half digested in the owl's stomach, had not ended so much as spread itself out as its vital energy transitioned away, atom by atom, each chunk the size of a baby caterpillar's bite. I felt it in my own body—not the objects but the animating energy passing through. It made me feel a bit sick. Butterflies.

The teacher had told us to report to him if we found worms in our pellets: clothes moths, he said. "They eat fur and feathers but they also love school uniforms, yum yum." He was one of those who speak to children as to idiots. But he still had his back turned to me and so I turned back to my desk. Then Lyona squealed and my hand jerked and knocked the pellet into two separate dry clumps. Something new poked out of one of them. It was white and still. There was a piece of fluff stuck to one side.

"Bone." I hadn't meant to say it aloud.

The teacher came immediately to my desk. "Great to see that some of our ladies aren't squeamish," he said in Lyona's direction. He crouched down beside me and grinned as though we were pals. I didn't like being called *ladies*, it was a word adults used when groups of girls were doing something wrong.

"What do we have here?"

The others around me were all looking now. I felt embarrassed by my filthy caterpillar. I pointed half-heartedly with the scalpel.

The teacher squinted into my magnifying glass, then stood up quickly, brushing his hands around the pockets of his trousers though it wasn't dusty.

"That isn't from your pellet. Where did you get it?"

I stared back at him and waited for an ally in the classroom to create some friendly distraction, but there was nobody there.

"You're not supposed to look at just anything that crawls across your desk."

I shrugged. I could look at any bit of the classroom and I'd see the same thing. Before I could protect the caterpillar the teacher brushed it with the outer edge of his little finger and it smudged into the desk.

"Now," he said in the same jocular tone. He used a pair of tweezers to move the tiny bone onto the sheet of paper entitled *Key* which was lying on my desk. On the paper, there were printed images of other tiny bones, teeth, claws, and feathers.

My tiny bone was set with tinier teeth. The teacher removed one with his tweezers. "This has no root," he said, "so what's that, then?"

I looked at him and he looked at me. He raised his eyebrows. "Hm?"

I said nothing. The teacher took the sheet of paper between finger and thumb and allowed it to shake, very slightly, until I looked.

"All you have to do is read it," he said. With great effort, he smiled.

Eventually I recognized my bone's square teeth in a picture on the Key and said that it was a vole.

"It's pulling teeth with you lot, ha!" he said. "I've never taught such a slow class." After that we all worked in silence for a while, heads down over the shit on our desks.

The bus was half full on the way home, secondary school had not yet gone back. It was a hot day, the leaves were still green, apples red on the trees along the road.

I walked home from the bus stop with Adam, Clare's younger brother, who talked in long cascades, which made little space for conversation. He was telling me about the diary he was keeping in which he recorded everything he did that day—everything including cleaning his teeth, and how he was planning to take it into school for show-and-tell, but this made him remember his Swiss Army knife, which he'd taken to the previous show-and-tell, and every one of its blades . . . He couldn't stop when we reached the gate and so I stood there, as I often did, thumbs looped into my backpack straps, waiting for a break in his streaming thought.

At the top of the lawn, at the side of the house, Clare was sitting in a chair with her feet in a paddling pool. She looked grown up. She mirrored Nic, facing her on an identical chair on the other side of the pool. Nic waved at me and I walked up the path to say hello.

Clare had been fed on cake and cherryade, doctor's orders, all summer, and she had filled out, a little, but her face was still hollow. She looked fragile, as I approached, until she waved merrily at me and said "Hiiiiiiiii," as though she was imitating or mocking me. I sifted my mind for something tactful to say, but Clare spoke before I could settle on the right thing.

"Nice woolly tights." She guffawed.

I looked down at my legs. They were thick and bright purple, wrinkled at the ankle. My mother had laid out warm clothing, ignoring the heat outside, because it was the autumn term. They were children's tights—not the tissue thin opaque tights that adult women wore. Women who laid out their own outfits. They were saggy and bobbly. The heat in my hot legs flowed up through my body and burned out in my face, but Clare, laughing, looked hard into my eyes as though we were sharing a joke that nobody else understood and then I started laughing, because I'd worn those tights all day without knowing how embarrassing they were, because I hadn't been aware that tights actually mattered or how much, because my mother was wrong, and because Clare was laughing, and because and because, and because, and then it was bleak but we were still laughing. Suddenly, Clare stopped. She stabbed a finger in the air. "Are you taking Adam swimming, then?"

I looked in the direction she was pointing. The hill, with the river on the other side of it.

"He's not allowed on his own and I'm too weak to walk it," she said matter-of-factly. "He wants to go."

I nodded. Clare smiled and tilted her head. "Go on, then," she said.

THERE WAS ALREADY A GROUP down at the river and I left Adam with the rest of them. It was hot but I hadn't jumped off the bridge since a boy from one of the farms had jumped into a piece of underwater scaffolding, which hadn't been taken down properly after the last time the bridge was repaired. He smashed a kneecap.

I wandered up the slope and climbed over the fence into the grounds of the abbey, following the line of a foot-wide stream of water which was channeled down to the river in a stone gutter. The line ended in the abbey grounds, at a large oblong zinc trough which had a constant stream of water slopping smoothly over its lip— the spring.

There was deep dense vibrant green watercress growing around the edges of the trough which was tall, the rim chest-high for me. I submerged my fingertips. The trough stood in full sun but the water, emerging from deep underground, was icy. I allowed my hands, then my wrists, to disappear. The cold was a relief. Tiny bubbles appeared on the surface of my skin, like in a fizzy drink. My arm went in and then my elbow, each area of skin paling as it was submerged and then crusting with tiny bubbles as though freezing to the spot.

There was a bang like a gunshot behind me. I turned, drying my hands on my top, but it was only a vehicle backfiring—a big old Land Rover, creamy-colored with rust patches. The ghost car. Thomas Gray was in the driver's seat. The passenger door opened and a woman, white-blond hair, fell out, shrieking with laughter. The woman was familiar to me but I couldn't place her. She screamed as though pretending to be horrified and then laughed wildly again, jumped free of the car, leaving the passenger door hanging wide. The engine was still running. She jumped over the abbey fence, kicked the honesty box so that it rattled, and shrieked with laughter again. She jogged toward me.

When she reached the spring I saw that it was Cat, the firewoman, though she looked different—her hair was longer and she was red-faced, breathless. She was still chuckling to herself. She plunged her bare arms into the water, splashed her face, and then said "Fuck it" and dunked her whole head in, pulled it out, dripping like waterweed, and twisted the water out of it as you would a wet towel. Then she pulled off her trainers, threw them on the grass, and climbed right into the trough. Water splurged over the edge and surged across the grass, trickling up to and over my feet. Cat stood tall, still wearing her vest and shorts, held her nose, then dropped to crouching, so that her whole body was underwater. Then she chuted up out like a whale breaking the surface. She staggered as she climbed out and ran back to the car with her dry shoes in her hands. The spring's water level had dropped but it was already replenishing itself.

Mr. Gray was in the driver's seat, hands on the wheel, the engine still turning over. Both windows were open. He waved at me by lifting his index finger from the steering wheel. He had a faint smile on his face, as though he recognized me from somewhere but couldn't place me, and for the first time I saw how much he looked like his mother. His vague smile was hers, standing in her warm kitchen, smiling into the air. It made me see how different the two of them were.

Cat stood on the side of the road and circled her head as though she was in a shampoo ad. Globes of water flew out of her long wet hair up into the sky and then they dropped small dark circles on the tarmac. Cat jumped into the car, whooped, and hit the side of her door with the flat of her hand. "Go." The car jolted forward.

The hill which climbed up the other side of the valley was steep. The Land Rover groaned loudly up it and screeched at the bend before the sound disappeared. After they had left, the environment was eerily quiet. A pheasant screeched in response to the car. Other sounds returned piecemeal, as though individually creeping back, and gentleness asserted itself in their wake. I could hear three continuous and distinct sounds, held together in the same place like strands in a plait. I could hear the river, out of sight, and the voices of the other children blended into it. I could hear the faded sound of the freeway running along, low. And separately, nearby, the sound of the spring, which was the gentlest sound. When I looked back into the spring its surface had returned to what it was—smooth, with a varying bulge at one end above the point at which the water issued out of the ground, spilling smoothly over the edge of the zinc tank at the other side. Below the surface the disturbance was still visible. Some of the bright green watercress at the side had been pushed under and there was a fat column of disturbed mud within the bright water. I felt nervous. I told myself that I hadn't seen anything. A car that wanted fixing and a woman laughing. But Cat's mood and Mr. Gray's glazed greeting put me on edge. I had been taught that everything has to be paid for and there was something inside me, learned or deeply known, which applied this principle to experience too—that I had to be wary of joy, like those poisonous fish which are delicious in small amounts and deadly when consumed at scale. Each giddy shrieking laugh spent a little of the life force, added a zero to the debt. Cat's drenched shining body exhibited the spring, which continued to make the noise it had been making for the whole hour, before, after, and during the period when its sound was drowned out, and before that, running and running, before I was there and long before that, years, millennia, luring monks then peasants then farmers then quarry workers, and for every second, throughout that time, it had been sustaining this stream of water. The stream was only the size and strength of a running tap but so persistent, in its modest way, that it must have passed a tsunami through the valley over the years.

One year the river choked up with green waterweed. I recognized the plant, though I hadn't learned its name, because I had seen it in Matthew's garden pond where it released oxygen and had snails with pointed shells climbing all over it. The weed was coarse rather than slimy in the river, so at first it wasn't too nasty to swim or paddle in it, but after a while it became so thick that there was a putrid feeling when I kicked through the water and tentacles spiraled around my legs. I don't know how it was for the fish. Maybe they made use of the extra cover to conceal themselves from the heron, or it's possible that the oxygen suffocated them. In summer the weeds expanded into massed tangles, each stem fragmenting into a hundred new organisms but doing so only lazily, hardly moving in the cool, clear, slow water. In winter when the river froze thick I could see the weeds framed inside the ice. They held their color for months, sitting out on life until spring. They looked good like that.

It was in this still state, when the water was frozen and the weeds' lives were on pause, that I saw them as trailing locks of human hair. In summer the weeds were animated, but it was their own weedy animation and they didn't look humanoid to me. But in the winter, under ice—I had heard stories of women trapped inside swamps who would grasp your shin, pull you down, and drown you.

This story was passed between children in the playground or in the graveyard after school. Anything supernatural was told like this: we had to sit in a close circle with coats over our heads to block out the surroundings and the light. The stories which were told were not original—they were what is known as urban myths, though there wasn't so much that was urban as we told them. There was a woman in the village, you see, she lived in one of the bungalows off the back road. She was scared of her violent ex, she had a restraining order against him but he still came over sometimes after a few and stood outside her house shouting, and so she bought an Alsatian puppy, like Paul Hodsman's dad did after he had the horses stolen. The woman's puppy was a beauty, warm and friendly and fluffy, but protective of her too, and he grew huge. The woman felt safe when her dog was there. While he was little he slept on her bed, but he grew too big so he started sleeping under the bed. She put a blanket down there for him. Then one evening the ex rang. He was drunk again and he threatened her. The woman closed all the windows in her house. She double-locked the front door and closed the second door firm. The front doors in those bungalows are made of glass. They have the porch, and then a second door behind them. There was a storm that night. The woman woke up with every flicker and bang and she put her hand under the bed. Her dog licked her, warm and reassuring, and she found that she could go back to sleep.

Then she heard a strange noise. She woke up, put her hand down, and the dog licked her hand again. Feeling stronger and bolder she went downstairs and whistled for him to come behind her. The frosted glass in the front door had smashed. Perhaps it had been hit by lightning, or something had fallen into it in the storm. There was nothing to be done until morning. She closed and bolted the inner door and went back to bed, still in the dark. She checked that the dog was there and he licked her hand. A few minutes later there was a crash downstairs and she went down again. This time she switched on the light. The dog's dead body was on the kitchen table and written in its blood on her wall were the words *Men can lick too*. She turned around and her ex was there. He fucked her, then he killed her, and then he fucked her again.

There was another woman whose husband was not that bad. She had come from out more toward Scarborough and she lived between the villages. An axe-murderer had escaped from prison and they said that he was hiding in a rural area, there were rumors that he was in the woods behind Mr. Gray's farm, sleeping rough. People knew he was there because badgers had been found with their heads cut off. This murderer decapitated things for a laugh.

The couple—the woman and her husband—were driving home late from a party in town when the car broke down on the road, only a few miles from the quarry and the edge of the village, but the weather was bad, sheeting it. The man climbed out to look into the engine. Don't get out of the car, he told his wife. She clicked down the central locking system. The hood of the car went up and her husband disappeared behind it. She waited. It was dark, and she couldn't see far through the heavy rain. A few minutes passed. Then a few more. There was a tapping sound. Her husband, she thought, must have found the problem in the engine. The tapping paused, then began again. Tap, tap, tap. The woman waited. The rain poured down. She could see nothing. Tap, tap, tap. Then another pause. She felt uneasy. Tap. Tap. Tap.

The woman felt more and more fear. She was angry with her husband for being so slow. Her last boyfriend had been better with cars. Tap, tap, tap. The noise was annoying her now, the rain going on and on. She didn't like it, being trapped in the dark car—she could as well walk. She pulled the door handle but the central lock was still on. She unlocked the car, jumped out and slammed the door, and then she turned around. There, sitting cross-legged on the roof of the car, was a man she had never seen before. This man was holding a stick, and on the end of the stick, impaled through the eye socket, was her husband's bloodied head, which was being tapped on the bodywork. Tap, tap, tap.

These stories were useful and sensible. They revealed a disturbingly interesting world beyond my perception, and they taught me that my senses and my intelligence wouldn't always read everything right. Still, the delicious plummet of fear through my chest in the playground felt different at midnight when the horror was more of a fact. I woke up and could hear cracking, humming, rustling, and breathing all around, my sleeping parents, hunting foxes, electricity cables, wind in the wheat, engines, air currents licking and whispering to one another, all indistinguishable from one another and continuous with pure evil.

For as long as I've been isolating, I haven't felt that the disease out there in the world is real, but I haven't seen the woman in the window opposite for two days now and this morning there was an ambulance outside her building. She must have tested positive. They say that it feels just like the flu at first, but then it slowly starves you of breath. I wonder how old she is. The man she lives with, who I assume is her partner, is still feeding his tomatoes as though nothing has happened, but he's on his own in there now. He's moved her sewing machine away from the window.

Opposite him, at my window, there's a stream of ants. They've run right up the side of the building and their road runs across my window box, between the geraniums. The ants can come in through the window even when it's closed, they're small enough. There are not many inside the building. I looked them up and they're harmless to plants, though they might nip a human. When I sit back at my desk I feel as though I am miles above them in an entirely different world, but when I get right down on the floor to watch them I am there with them, making a living chain, each one taking its direction from the ant in front of it. Sometimes one will turn back and beckon the others with its antennae.

In winter, when the waterweed was frozen inside the ice over the river, I saw the pale hair of the dead woman who was waiting to trap me. And then one day there she was, standing on the surface of the ice. A strange pale human figure, right out in the middle. She was dressed in a white coat, with a Russian white fur hat, and she was wheeling a huge old-fashioned baby carriage. The carriage was fancy, navy blue with white piping. The woman with her heavy carriage was walking on the ice over the river, so that the wheels traced rail shapes in a circle on the surface. She was walking, in very small steps, slowly, in a wide circle right across the river, over the site of the bulrushes, around the edges and out over the center, where the current beneath her would be pushing at its most powerful and where, in summer, the water sparkled with escaped sunlight, and she continued, stepping slowly, toward the alders on the opposite bank, where she smoothly turned and walked down beside the bank before striking out again into the middle, over the thinnest ice. The wheels were creaking, or perhaps it was the ice groaning below her weight.

Her narrow form sent a clutch of white fear into me but my body kept on walking steadily toward her. When I reached her I recognized her. It was Ms. Carr with her new baby. A daughter. We had made cards at school. That day Ms. Carr did not have a bruise on her face, or a broken arm, or even the bandages taping two of her fingers together, more than once the same two. Nonetheless, or perhaps because of this, there was something odd about her. Her eyes were lowered, her face uninhabited. She greeted me by my full name crisply, in a low voice, without looking up and without pausing on her circuit. The baby carriage wheeled. The ice creaked. She asked me for the news at school and I said that everything was fine and she said that that was good.

I waited for a while. The hood was up on the baby carriage. "What are you doing?"

"The baby is going to sleep," she said. The baby carriage was a dark, hooded form bending over the baby and I couldn't see it. Ms. Carr followed the curve of her course so that her back was turned to me and I watched her, stepping steadily. Clicks and groans rose out of the ice, the rusty wheels, and her court shoes striking the hard surface. The valley cradled the sounds. I turned around and walked away, to give her peace, and I was surprised by the sharp edge of my own disappointment. I wanted to look at the baby.

I walked the mile up the road to my house. It was uphill, and covered at the steepest inclines with a thick and smooth glazing of black ice. I tired, walking it, and sat down in the turnout marked PASSING PLACE. Below me the valley was stylish and reserved, fiercely focused on wintriness, white and pine green, frost-tipped needles still hanging onto the very ends of larch branches in the deeply frozen quiet. From here I could see the shape of the river, which had tributaries and sideslips eddying into it, which I couldn't see from close up, where the river appeared to me as one steady flowing mass, disappearing to my right into a white sky and merging to my left with the white distance, so that I felt cocooned inside it. My face was warm with the effort of walking up the hill, but I was cold and wet where my bum rested on the frozen tarmac, I felt myself leaking body heat into this delicate, intent environment and it showed me what I was *about*, in the way a story is about something and sometimes, as you read something meandering, feeling bewildered and a little bit annoyed for a long time, you suddenly catch a glimpse of a point—*the* point—that playing my Game Boy, or eating soup, or talking to Ms. Carr was where I was a part of the winter. On the opposite hillside a pretty blue metal snake slid along a railing, winked gold, and disappeared. The train track, which looked like a toy, had been laid out to connect the coasts to the cities, the outskirts to the center, but the dream was dead, its sleepers led nowhere except on a day trip to visit an elderly relative in one of the long avenues of old boarding houses in Scarborough that had been fitted out as nursing homes. It was so quiet in the valley that I could still hear Ms. Carr's baby carriage wheels rumbling across the ice, though she was a long way out of sight.

I'd stood on that road on a summer day when the stillness and heat made me aware of how far inland I was, away from breezes and waves of dense, cold salty water. Around noon I was walking up from the river and the heat baked the surface so that spots of black tar rose in strings like chewing gum on my heel. The boring sun had stalled above me and time seemed to stop, and it only restarted with the rhythm of heavy boots falling.

I turned and saw, down the slope, a group of men in tight mud-green t-shirts with huge muscular thighs swelling out of their shorts. The men were ranked in straight rows, three abreast, and they took the steep hill at a run. The clanking sound came from the aluminum drinks bottles and small pans that were clipped onto the outsides of their overstuffed green backpacks. As a whole, the physical power of this running machine was awesome. It occupied the narrow lane. I was in its path.

I moved into the turnout and flattened my back against the high verge, beneath the PASSING PLACE sign, so that the machine could get through. It pushed a heated breeze in front of it. Heavy breathing, raw-shaven faces and bare skulls pricked with shaven hair. Occasionally, a deep sound dropping from a mouth. The simultaneous drop and drop and drop of heavy soles. Real war was far away. On television it looked much easier than these training exercises. People danced on tanks, in the street, and on a high wall. They kissed and danced some more as they emerged through forests into the outskirts of foreign towns. On the news it looked simple to bring peace and joy to the whole world, easy as passing a red-hot blade through butter, easy and gratuitous as a boy jogging along a road, liberating two feet of land with every step. Only the boy's real body, when it appeared as an intimidating physical presence, struggling under the pressure it was forcing onto itself, suggested that other things were happening in some desert at the back of my mind, in a place which had been emptied of living connection or content, where a tank sat static in miles and miles of lunar landscape. Grey sand, strewn with the occasional boulder. The news showed the tank sitting, and sitting, and then suddenly it rocked with fire which jolted its body like a belch. Then it returned to sitting. This was the reality of war—this was what the boys were in rehearsal for when they strained along the hawthorn hedges and past the post office, out by the field where Rebecca's ponies looked up from grazing, and then along the quarry road, past the quarry which was no longer operating, the machinery parked at the top of the track.

It was unusual to see a group of young men together. There were children in school and there were old men in the village, but there weren't many men of football-playing age, and those who remained lived the mostly solitary lives of a young farmer or of an adult boy who lives with his parents while waiting for work to find him. John Green's older brother Lee had gone straight from school to work on an oil rig so that he could dodge the inheritance of his dad's farm. Paul, who was the actual nephew of the neighbor I called Auntie Pauline, left home in the early hours, without telling his family where he was going, but a few days later he rang from a city down south, where he'd found a job in an electronics shop. There was once a limp campaign for a twice-daily bus service into the city. It would have changed the constitution of the place, but the people who were successful at making their voices heard were also the people who owned cars. The campaign never went anywhere and the slow drain continued.

Canadian machines had drained the quarry beautifully and the company had cut down deep to extract better, and more. The quarry had widened at the base so that the walls now leaned in above the opening. When I stood at the bottom and looked up, this new form was psychedelic, I had the impression that the leaning walls were on the brink of falling in on me. From above, though, the widening depths were obscured by vegetation: huge ferns which plugged themselves into the smallest recesses, extended out from the sides. The Canadians still owned the quarry but they had halted production. The only work there now was maintenance, carried out every quarter or so, on the small area of quarry that was still workable. The earth was always damp down there. One day I found a tiny toad. His legs made him visible, spread digits filigree against some wet white fallen cherry blossoms, and I bent my head down close to him to look. He was smooth and damp, a very dark khaki color with a gold sheen. He was teeny. If he had driven a car it would have been the size of an acorn.

The toad was on his way somewhere and my looming face didn't deter him from his mission. He moved by extending one crooked arm at a time and then dragging his body forward. His legs seemed to do little work. It was a curious movement and it made me think of a few moments of a film I'd glimpsed on the television, in which a young soldier whose legs had been blown off used his arms to haul himself away from the battle zone, dragging bleeding stumps behind him. Likewise, the toad advanced painstakingly over the fallen blossom. Each soggy petal, stacked and folded into the others, in a rut at the base of a piece of broken rock, was an obstacle. He reached the base of the rock and put his upper hand on the vertical side.

One face of this rock was sheer and slippery with wet. The other side was rubblier. I could see the regular marks where it had been cut with blades, and the uneven surface where it had ripped from the surrounding stone. The toad was attempting the slippery vertical cut side and I thought that he would unstick and roll back down but he didn't, he plodded up the vertical line, over a patch of darker striations, where he slipped and I saw his front arms skid. His whole body collapsed into his haunches, which held fast. Slowly, blinking, he began cautiously to crawl forward again, and moved steadily at a reduced pace until he reached the top. At the summit of the rock there was a small hump and the toad could not get over it. He tried to reach but his arm could not extend far enough. He tried to climb around the side but the angle was too steep. He was unable to retreat, unless he climbed backward, and this would have meant using the back legs and they seemed to contain strength without mobility. He overbalanced and flipped backward, landing with his soft underbelly exposed, in the place where I had seen him start. Instinctively I looked upward. It was a cool pearly day in early summer. The sky was blanked out with an even spread of silver cloud. The walls loomed down on us, the thin leaves of the weeds growing out of the quarry walls wavered very slightly. When I looked back down the toad was on his feet again and already beginning to climb. I watched him cover the distance of the rock, one tiny arm's length after another. When finally he achieved the summit for the second time he paused for a long moment. My body was suspended inside his decision. Slowly he re-angled his body with mechanical laboriousness, inching fractionally from one orientation to the next. He looked smooth and agile, fishlike, when he crawled around the edge of the hump. He began to descend the other side.

I crouched down, squatting froglike with my fingertips on the floor, and followed his path with my eyes until he reached the bottom. He stretched out his leg and continued to move in the same straight line, onward, across the quarry floor. Then I felt the slightest ache in my knee, a flattening of the light, and I knew that soon I would become bored. I wanted to know where the toad was going but I also felt a mounting conviction that he was not going anywhere. I could see where his path was leading, a long way into his future. Nothing over there, on the other side of the quarry bed, was much different to this place, here, where we were. I felt frustration arise in my body. I felt certain that he had some destination in mind, or that the north side of the quarry *meant something* to the toad and I did not have the patience to wait and see where it was. Out of the corner of my eye I noticed a slight, stiff movement somewhere in front of the toad. It was another tiny toad, his face turned at precisely the same angle, advancing in exactly the same direction. When I scanned the ground around them, I picked up a movement here, and here, and here. The empty ground animated itself. The damp stony floor of the quarry was teeming with baby toads. Each one was angled in precisely the same direction, moving diagonally across the quarry, and each one was engaged in his own personal slow advance. I crouched down again and watched them all for a while. I allowed myself to be interested in their mission without understanding it and I found, to a slowly dawning sense of surprise, that the experience of being interested in this journey, this toad, this migration, was relaxing.

I didn't think about what the baby toads were doing down at the bottom of the quarry or how they had got there down the vertical sides. I did not step back to look around me or learn or think properly about the facts of life, and so it didn't occur to me that the baby toads were making their first exodus from a body of water. The nearest source that I knew of was the creek which ran along the bottom of the valley inside the wood and was only a short distance away, but the terrain was uneven, up the walls of the quarry, along the footpaths, and then plunging down a steep slope. I was looking from the path down that slope one early summer evening when I realized I had never set foot down there. It was twilight, there was a blue gloom suspended through the air before me, and one small spot of glowing substance somewhere deeper in among the trees, small as a candle flame. I sat down on a fallen branch and squinted toward it. The evening gave me a feeling of quiet promise, something easing and shifting as it does in a pub in late afternoon. Darkness settles lightly and with calm. Diurnal creatures return to their beds and roosts, and night begins. Deep in the wood another light shone out. Dimly, fitfully, the space self-lit. Fireflies. Their faint, wavering lights made negative space come to life, each glimmer an indicator, each indicator making demonstration of a small orb of room between the trees. I was aware that there was something sticky beneath my bare knee and when I stood up there was a dark resinous substance on the back of my leg.

The branch I was sitting on was, in fact, a broken wooden post as thick as a railway sleeper, half in and half detached from the earth like a broken tooth. The broken part was ragged and damply splintered and it was covered with several of these dark blobs. The light given off by the distant fireflies was not good. I couldn't see what the blobs were. I sat down on the ground beside the post, in the middle of the footpath which wasn't often used, and leaned my back against the upright part of the stake while I cleaned my leg with a garlic leaf, and then regretted the stink. Behind me the light sky was divided into a geometric grid with liquid black lines. It took a moment for me to see the silhouette of a wire fence, neatly posted at regular intervals with new, thinner stakes. An old footpath ran along the fence, along the top of the bank—the wood dropped steeply to the right. I had never walked off the path and down that slope to the bottom of the wood: it dropped too quickly to be comfortably navigated with shoes, though I could probably have slid down it on my bum. As I sat there, looking down, time passed slowly, the blue deepened and my eyes adjusted, I could feel my pupils expanding, and I began to hear a low humming sound. When I looked up I couldn't see anything. The sound seemed to be coming from a tree. It was too dark to see the tree in detail, it was inked on the sky. Then I saw a black dot drift away from the tree. I watched it floating slowly, I thought perhaps it was a seed but no, it had small, transparent wings. Then I thought it must be a firefly but there was no glow. Another black dot appeared from the gloom and floated toward the tree, where it was eclipsed by, or disappeared into, a small circular craft the size of a ping-pong ball which rested at the fork of two twigs, up high.

It was a puzzle. I scanned the area around me and I saw that there were long pale scratches up the base of the trunk, as though somebody had skinned a line in the greenish surface with a fingernail, and in the surrounding area, all together, I saw dim hoofprints pressed into the earth, a tangle of coarse hairs on the base of the wire fence, and a smooth depression below it in the earth where the bodies wiggled through, desire paths fading away from this entrance or exit over which the weeds dangled as the trees overhung my path, concealing the travelers from hawks' eyes. I followed this miniature path with my eyes. It passed up the knee-high wall of earth, mossed over and collapsed in places, which ran in a broken line around the edge of the wood. The old boundary had been forgotten by people but it was maintained in the ground as a physical memory of all these different times, nocturnal, historical, ordinary, futuristic, present. I heard a twig snap and turned. A face appeared in a hole on the side of the slope. A fox cub.

The cub emerged, sniffing the dusk. It disappeared, then reappeared in glimpses between trees. A few moments later another two cubs appeared and a thin adult fox behind them. The mother was bony, with pale fluff around her face. She moved with a limping motion. At first I thought she had an injured leg, but then she lay down and two cubs came to feed, I could see that she was swollen with milk. It was becoming too dark to see and I had to go home. I left without disturbing them.

The next day I went into the wood while it was still daylight. When I looked closely at the scratches in the bark of the nearby tree, the relief revealed the living wood, forms emerging within the material as the wood chips inside the wallpaper at home showed themselves up in artificial light. Badgers perhaps. But the scratches ran up the trunk, rising above a badger's head, above mine, and on up into the air, where, resting lightly between the branches of the tree, there was a tiny spherical planet made entirely of pale lacy grey paper and wasps, drifting lazily in and out of it. The sky was full of light: I could see their stripes. When I looked down, twilight was gathering at my feet. I recognized something on the ground, blue flowers slowly dissolving into the bluing air. The wood anemones had spread throughout the forest, pushing the wild garlic back behind their front line. I remembered that I had seen a tiny pool of wood anemones, holding together in a sea of wild garlic, years earlier when I sat on the gate waiting for Mr. Gray's escaped cows to come charging past me. Since then, slowly, steadily, rhizome by rhizome feeling through the earth, the anemones had spread. It must have been an incremental advance, the fragile flowers' strangling of the other plants hardly noticeable at the time. Now they were blooming in palest blue, hanging their heads with a modesty which denied the fact that they had taken over and they weren't going anywhere; they were everywhere. They had won. They had taken the space from the garlic, which had carpeted the wood in earlier years but was pushed back now into isolated zones, and thinning. I leaned my back against the tree trunk and slid down, the friction between my vertebrae and the mossy trunk burned a mark on my back. I was closer to the foxhole that time.

When the fox cubs emerged, I watched them for a while. I thought of them all as boys. Two played violent games with one another: the larger bit the smaller by the scruff of the neck and then rolled the smaller body over his shoulders. The third cub had a gentler spirit. He tucked his body into the vegetation so that leaves of anemones, garlic, and ground elder roofed over his haunches. His face peeped out, resting chin on paws philosophically while his siblings played. I could see how blue his eyes were and I could follow the gaze when his head cocked and twitched from side to side, mirroring the jerking of a flying insect, somewhere in the air beside him, which I couldn't see. My leg was slowly going dead and I had to shift my weight. Immediately, with the sound, the smallest fox-cub shot back into the tunnel. The mother took his companion in her mouth, by the scruff, and carried him quickly into the foxhole. She disappeared for a moment, and I thought that she had forgotten about the third cub, who was still sitting calmly at the edge of the clearing, gazing with his chin on his paws. But the mother appeared again. When she went to fetch him, the cub twisted around so that she was forced to open her jaws and let him drop. The cub returned to his former position, lying on the edge of the clearing, looking in. The mother went again to pick him up. There was a snap and the mother yelped, for a second the cub was hanging from her muzzle by his jaws. He was big, more solidly built than she was. He dropped down again and returned to the position in which he had determined to sit.

The mother turned around then and faced me directly. I could see her intelligence working and hear her inhalations. She had a decision to make. Her muzzle tilted upward to research our environment. Then she settled back down beside her cub, though her eyes were still wide open and her nose alert to the air. I felt a moment of misconnection, like the moment when somebody waves to you and you wave back, then you glance over your shoulder and you see that their greeting was intended for somebody behind you. I was the danger. The danger was me. I sat as quietly as I could and a long time later the other cubs came out again and resumed their play.

I watched the cubs play there several times through the spring. They grew quickly, which impressed me, waiting as I always was for my own next birthday. They learned to stalk and pounce, practicing on one another, on moths, and, once, on a stunned wagtail that their mother brought back as a living toy. When at last the bird was dead the mother buried it in a shallow grave with one wing poking out, and the largest cub retrieved it a few moments later. Then they buried it again. That was fun for them.

Occasionally I made an inadvertent noise, snapped a twig, or stifled a cough. When this happened the foxes melted away and only rarely reappeared before I went home. One evening, after I'd been visiting for a while, I accidentally scraped loose some earth which skittered in dry balls down the slope and bounced right into the middle of the foxes, landing at their feet. The cubs pounced on the moving pieces of dirt but the mother froze and turned to look at me with her pointed face. I held my breath, waited for her to usher them all down into the ground. The transaction of earth from my feet to theirs unsettled me, as though I had passed a cup of tea through my television screen and a character inside had picked it up and taken a sip. The mother gave me a hard look, the pale fuzz around her face haloing her weirdly. Then she relaxed and settled, arching her neck to nip a mite on her shoulder.

So the fox family began to tolerate me and I knew that it wasn't my presence which made them freeze, then bolt back into their earth, another evening when I hadn't, in any case, made noise. I couldn't hear anything. Something told me to turn around, slowly, making no sudden movement. Behind me, only a few paces away, there was a huge fox balanced with all four legs on the broken beam. Perhaps it was because I had become accustomed to the sight of the skinny mother and her cubs, but this creature looked to me more tiger than fox. His tail was broad and sleek, his shoulders heavy. Even in twilight, his coat glinted with red points. He was simultaneously smelling the stake I had sat on before and rubbing himself on it with the two ends of his body. His posture was adoring and abject, he wrapped himself around the stake as a cat wraps herself around the legs of those who have access to cat food. Gradually, an intense musky scent pervaded the air around me. I realized what it was I'd got on my leg that time and I realized that this fox could not be the only fox who adored this stake, which had lost its point and its place within a human border and gone feral, collapsed into alternative organizations of space. It soaked up traces of everything it weathered and all the bodies who passed it, who used it to find out where they were, and to tell others that they were, would be, or had been, present. Then the huge fox elegantly made his way to the end, strained on his haunches, and shat. It wasn't so different, in its place, to a form of human domination, which articulates itself in the flow of toxic effluent from the most powerful bodies and corporations through pipes, outlets, dumps, and treatment plants, into the places where the most vulnerable make their homes. In the silence after the dog fox left I could hear the wasps, scraping the bark from the tree, turning it into their grey tissue.

One day, later, the vixen changed. She was bothered by something—fretful—she kept moving the cubs even though they were too big to be carried easily. She picked up one cub and moved him to the other side of the clearing. Then she returned to chase another cub down into the foxhole. She moved in an agitated way, occasionally shaking her body as though she needed to get water out of her fur. She returned again to collect the cub she had dropped on the edge of the clearing. With a sinking sensation, I watched her move him back to his initial position. Patches of her back twitched, revealing muscles like tectonic plates beneath her hide. Her ears were flicking constantly. The cubs showed no sign of distress that I could see. They allowed their bodies to go limp so that their mother could pick them up and move them around, and then, when she left them alone, calmly they resumed activities. I felt alienated from them. It was possible that they simply did not notice the change that had come over their mother. Or, they were responding, but the response took place in some private communication that was inaccessible to me. I did not know which possibility was the more disturbing. I looked around but could make out no immediate danger. The cubs did not—could not—show emotions as expressions on their faces.

A few nights later, when the cubs appeared, there was a pool of bright blue liquid with foam around its edges at the foot of a nearby tree. It smelled rank. The cubs sniffed at this blue puddle but they didn't lick it. I waited, but the mother didn't appear at all.

By the end of the week the cubs too were acting strangely. They moved more slowly, drowsily, and they seemed unfocused. When they pounced on insects, they missed. They chewed on sticks and leaf mold, perhaps trying to get at worms or woodlice. The two larger cubs playfully nosed their brother to the ground. The smallest cub lay out flat, as their mother had, and his brother nosed into his belly and sucked. Then the other brother took a turn. The fruitless sucking made a draining sound, like a drinking straw pulling on dregs. They did not stop trying.

This became their new game. The mother did not reappear, and the cubs were older now but they did not leave their home. A physical weakness was becoming apparent on their bodies, taller, thinner. They no longer played so physically with one another, their movements had become clumsily languid. They lay separately in their clearing, pushing leaf mold under their paws or simply resting, each one alone in his mind. Sometimes the two larger cubs would gently nose the smallest to the ground and try to feed from the incipient organ that was developing on his underbelly.

Over time, his fur came out in patches. When he came out of the earth he often stumbled over the large protruding root that ran across the opening, and he spent his evenings lying in the middle of the clearing. I could see his breath rising and falling. When his siblings went to feed from him he no longer turned, but they rolled him over with their noses so that they could get to his underside. I could see, even from afar, that the belly was tightly inflated and inflamed. Still, he did nothing to prevent his brothers from feeding from the sore place, though his body occasionally responded to their touch by contracting, automatically, with a pulse of pain. He had a placid, faraway expression on his face, his eyes open but veiled. It was no surprise when, one evening, he did not emerge from the earth.

That same evening the largest cub ventured out into the wood on the far side of the clearing. No cub had ever gone so far before. He was crossing an invisible boundary which had always been respected. His form dissolved into the gloom between the trees, his frame solid and his tail thick: he was a young adult. A few minutes later he returned but the next night he was gone. Then there was only one cub left.

The last evening I visited, I sat for a long time with him. He had filled out since the days after his mother's disappearance. I watched him catch a moth by himself. He contained its batting form between his paws with dexterity and ate it alive. He seemed a little stronger and I thought that he would live.

The creek ran along the base of the slope below the foxhole. It was not picturesque, it was scummy, slowed to a trickle in summer with rotting twigs and litter, and there was no path. One day I was walking along it, following the curve of the water, which turned a corner; I climbed over a fallen tree and almost fell over a small brown nylon dome: a tent.

The door was open and I looked inside. The tent was empty other than an open sleeping bag, unzipped halfway down, and humped like a caterpillar at the foot end, so that it bore traces of movement, of being shaped by a body, and I felt a physical pang of pity or fear or love. There was a Gatorade bottle in front of the tent and a used cup of instant noodles with the stock crusted in the bottom. A large khaki backpack was leaning against a tree trunk. The man was standing up against a tree with his back to me, facing the trunk. He zipped up his flies as he turned around and then he saw me.

He had a shaven head and a bare face. When he caught sight of me, a deep blush spread across his cheekbones. He pulled his flies up again but the zip was already fully closed and didn't go any higher. He was old to me but not elderly, probably not yet in his twenties—he looked like John Green's brother Lee, who also had a shaven head and was about the same age. Lee came back from his job on the oil rig with all his fingers missing on one hand. A pipe had fallen between levels. At school, John said that the pipe had been *improperly installed*, and Shelley said Lee should claim compensation. John said: "They say it was Lee who installed it."

Shelley asked if they were lying and John shrugged. "He can't remember."

Shelley gave John a withering look. "He'll be back on the farm, then."

"As and when," said John mildly.

Shelley had arrived at school mid-term and took control of the playground because she was exceptionally pretty. She told us that she had already been to six schools and that her dad moved to work in a different place every year, it was something to do with the army, not soldiering. Shelley had learned from necessity that she had to seize power or remain alone. She wouldn't have been able to do it without her looks. Shelley's hair was long, her face was symmetrical, her skin almost unnoticeable, and her figure was already feminine. On her very first day all the girls in the year gathered around her to study her accessories and to listen to what she had to tell us. We learned that she was in possession of a body spray in Vanilla. Within days, every girl had or needed one of these body sprays and it would not be an exaggeration to say that it was dangerous to be without one that term. The body sprays came in slender cans with a pearly aerosol which released droplets of sugary mist. Vanilla, Peachy, and Summer Blossom were available. The cans were decorated with pictures of butterflies, peaches, or cherry trees, and for a few weeks these slim pretty objects were involved in everything, they contained every possibility that bodies on the brink of adolescence could imagine: we played with them as dolls, and we breathed in their contents, and we had a heightened awareness that the scent was a trailer for sex—or what we thought sex was. It smelled like broken sweets. Those of us who knew how to inhale would make this intense sweetness backflip in our throats, which made our eyes water, our ears ring, and skip our minds over. Then we'd be physically filled with laughter which surged out of us like spray from an aerosol. Girls who had no body spray at all were not worth thinking about. We all wanted to be more like Shelley and we understood that we could become more like her by having the possessions she had. We needed to smell like her. I chose Summer Blossom, not Vanilla as Shelley had, and it was lucky I did. One day I was with

Ann and Shelley in the schoolyard. We were playing—throwing the cans around in a circle—you had to throw one over to your left, and swing to catch the incoming from your right, so the cans all danced through the air at the same time, and for a few moments the three of us and our body sprays were in time, throwing, swinging, catching, and pausing, until Shelley threw one of the cans too hard so that it bounced off the wall behind Ann's shoulder and fell, badly dented, at our feet.

The broken can was Vanilla. My can of Summer Blossom was safe in my own hand. I closed my fingers around it.

Shelley snatched up the undamaged can of Vanilla. "That one's yours," she said to Ann, pointing her toe at the broken can.

"No," said Ann. She shoved Shelley gently and reached toward the intact can. Shelley held her arm outstretched behind her back.

One of the older girls was standing nearby, wearing the neon vest that identified a dinner monitor. The dinner monitor came over to see what was happening. Shelley explained in her prettiest voice that the fight had arisen because there were two identical body sprays and one had broken. Who now should take it home? The dinner monitor drew herself up.

"I think it was mine," said Ann.

"I'm sorry," said Shelley, "it was mine."

The dinner monitor looked at the two cans, one dented, one apparently perfect, and then she looked at the two girls. At Shelley's beautiful innocent face and at Ann whose eyes were enlarged and agonized behind her glasses.

"Which one of you ladies is honest? It can't be both of you."

Suddenly, Ann sat right down on the concrete and dragged her fist hard across its surface.

"Whatever, give it to her, it's obvious who you'll choose."

Shelley pouted and looked away.

"I am not here for my own amusement," said the dinner monitor. She confiscated both cans and hid her hands behind her back. "Pick a hand."

Ann shook her torn knuckle and rose to leave. "Give it to her," she said dully. "Anyway she'll make my life difficult if I get it."

She rose to leave but the dinner monitor shook her head. "Not so fast, young lady. You wanted fair. Pick a hand."

Shelley rose, wiped her tears, and tapped the dinner monitor's left shoulder with blithe confidence. She was already in luck. "That one is mine."

There was a second's pause, during which the dinner monitor clumsily fiddled behind her back. One shoulder went down and the other rose as she unsubtly swapped the two cans from one hand to another. Then she moved her arms forward and opened her palms, holding out one arm to each small girl.

The perfect, undented can was handed to Ann.

"See?" said the dinner monitor triumphantly.

Ann glanced anxiously at Shelley and said quickly, "You have it."

Shelley was poorly equipped for the playground, but this was the only time I saw this impoverishment so cruelly exposed. She had been indulged or despised, in gratuity for her beauty or as revenge on it, for most of her time at my school—for most of her life, most likely. Her personality had twisted around the others' response to the way she looked. That day, faced with privation, she tilted her chin upward, an image of hard-won dignity, and gave Ann an adult, unreadable look, but she had no reserves of endurance. "I don't want it." She threw her battered can hard against the wall again and it exploded, a clear liquid dribbling out of the hole in its pearled plastic head as it rolled on the ground. At the end of term her family moved again.

In the woods behind his tent the man faced me squarely but he didn't approach. His cheeks flushed deeper as I held his gaze, but my eyes were drawn downward, toward the long wet stain he had made on the tree trunk.

"Go away," said the man. He had an accent like Ms. Carr's and he sounded older than he looked. Stern. He talked to me clearly, in the way that people give instructions to dogs, and he pointed up the slope. "Leave me alone." I ran.

I never heard about the man from anybody else, and I never told any adults he was there because I knew they would make a drama out of it. I didn't go back down there for a long time and when I did, at least a year later, he had gone. I found the exact place because his plastic noodle pot was still there, still in precisely the same position. The stock inside had been licked clean and the colored ink on the outside had faded away but the pot, solid ridged plastic like a small white skull, was still there, and in all likelihood is still there now, and will be there for ages after the man, and I, and all our contemporaries have gone. I find it difficult to believe that its every component was imagined into being: the noodle, the liquid plastic, the nest of dried corn threads that slotted into the circular shape, and the stratum of salted powder at the base, the plastic sachet of sauce, the scalloping on the pot, the green and yellow ink, the tiny image of a white-feathered chicken, and the looping font used for the logo, which gives an impression that it was handwritten, rather than printed, by a human being who was experiencing joy. All of it was invented and chosen. It was easy to be blind to it—not the original act of bringing pot noodles into being but the actual pot, which is just something which exists among all the forms and movements that surround me within and beyond my own narrow horizons, which, in my ordinary life, I overlooked. These days, living in an indoor world, I spend so much time looking on the same things that all their small details have crept into focus, moment after moment, not only the trademarks on the backs of the tins and packets inside my cupboards, whose contents I know completely, but also the shapes of the stains on the corrugated roof of the bin sheds outside the building opposite. Not only the shrubs whose names I don't know, but the individual buds on their right-hand branches, which opened a day or two earlier than the buds on the branches that reach out to the left, where they have to wait a few more minutes for the sun each morning. Not only each bud, but each of the tiny green tags inside it, developing, as though grudgingly, at an incremental pace. I wouldn't usually have the time or the patience to watch.

THE WOOD WASN'T BIG AND there was a proper track through it. People did not get lost in there. The only time I ever felt confusion was when I was on my way home from Stu Woodhead's birthday party. I have no memory of the party, or any childhood party in the singular, their common ritual practices have blended into one seamless sequence in my mind (dress, nerves, organized games, mounting excitement, cake, peaking excitement, party bags, overexcited weeping) but I remember the time I couldn't find this party, which was in a field at the edge of the wood, I was instructed to reach it by walking along the track. There were six Woodhead children living on the far side of the village in a small detached house with a long thin garden, with their car mechanic father and substitute teacher mother. Stu's mother had made a decision that she did not *do* housework, and so her home was a feral playground—more wild and exciting than the real outside because it occupied domestic space. The Woodheads' huge kitchen table was always covered across one half with newspaper on which small and heavy lumps of metal lay dimly gleaming through black grease. There was a fish tank full of deep green slime, through whose profundities trailed a huge white goldfish with a large growth on its back. The Woodheads ate food which was not much seen in the area—dark food—brown bread, rice, dried fruit. Food that took more chewing than children can be bothered with. But in that house any child could help herself, sawing the heel off a loaf with a huge serrated knife or spooning cement-hard peanut butter out of the white plastic bucket that sat on the side. I liked Stu's mother Yulia but I had the normal prejudices of my time, age, and place: I couldn't understand why she didn't just make her house look better. There was one room in particular, the television room, which had an atmosphere I didn't like. The room contained a television, sofa cushions, and a grubby curtain that had been pinned over the window. On the floor the spots and crusts of glue, and sharp tacks stuck into splinters of wood around the edges, drew attention to the absence of carpet. My distaste doesn't matter in itself, only in the fact that my thoughts were products of a world in which it was more common for a working woman to employ poorer women to clean up her dirt, than for her to let her floor carry glue spots. I liked Yulia. Occasionally she came into school as the special needs teacher and I'd see her sitting in the staff room with Richie and Kerry, the door wide open, doing sums on their fingers or bending over picture books. It looked happier than ordinary lessons. At school I was instructed to call her Mrs. Woodhead, which gave her first name a shine. She had that psychic capacity you see in mothers of many children, an ability to give her full attention to the next task, twenty seconds into the future. It would be easy to make a joke about her for being harried or haggard, which she was, or for the state of her house or her much-used body, but I found her attractive and unusually solid. Any child in her house was conscripted to the demands of the next event. She appeared out of nowhere. "Fetch me some raspberries for dinner, you can take a box home"—handing me a big bowl. "After that, wipe the table, and then you can go."

Her garden was the garden of some entirely different person who lived in another household, if not another world. It was precious. She grew roses with creamy petals marbled with red like raspberry ripple ice cream, artichokes, blue and white cornflowers. She grew tiny little cucumbers which she pickled in enormous jars. Her garden was the first place I saw a golden raspberry and a blueberry. She showed me how to choose the buckwheat berries, taking the brown and not the green, and to leave a little of everything for the birds and insects. In a parallel world there was another Yulia who had a large beautiful garden and a clean house with curtains waving in the breeze, and a single daughter neatly dressed with plaited hair and matching socks. A tidy life. In the real world, her maximal child-bearing had taken on a new meaning as her children grew up to a planet which had changed around them, with them, under them, which through them was reaching its capacity to bear life. In the community at the time there was disapproval of the family but it was not because of the overproduction of humans, it was because Stu Woodhead used to come to school in mismatching shoes two sizes too big for him and his sister's sparkly tights. He looked beautiful but he fell over all the time.

Adults did not directly or in public refer to Stu's look but he was always cast as an old woman in the Christmas play. He was quiet in class, he came into himself in character, onstage for the length of the play to offer commentary or distraction if the innkeeper leaked vomit through his nose while delivering his only line, if a lamb wandered offstage because its Nana was in the audience, or if Mary, tripping over her long dress, let out at the same time a small fart and a loud *Fuck*, which came out in a coarse voice that didn't sound like the odd warbling tone she adopted when speaking as the Mother of God. Any development would be met with something wise from Stu, who had gravitas in his second-hand wedding dress and judge's wig, tall, rail-thin, holding himself very still. He spoke with a quiet, laconic deliberation that acted as a metronome, slowing down the play which would, without him, have fallen over its own excitement, missed most cues, and ended in ten minutes. Then one year we did *Samson and Delilah*. Stu's Delilah wasn't pretty, her lower lip tended to hang loose as Stu's did in a way that suggested that her intelligence was less sharp than it was, but she was striking, with her angular masculine shoulders, her dark red lips, and thick, pointed black eyebrows.

On the night of the performance Stu looked very serious as he prepared. For a long time he sat still on a plastic classroom chair, topless, straight-backed, one hand on each knee. Dark lipstick, school trousers, a meditative stare. Ash and I were fixing paper crowns on one another's heads and Ash was laughing at me because the crown kept slipping right over my head to sit around my neck, like the plastic collars dogs wear to prevent them from biting their stitches. "You can be a camel instead," Ash said. I kicked him on the shin and Ms. Carr sent me out of the room to stand facing the wall outside the staff room, where I could reflect on my behavior.

I stood there for a while. Behind my back the others filed onto the stage. I wasn't allowed to turn around. Meanwhile I stared at the wall. Its minor cracks and marks swung in and out of focus, making sense, making a pattern, and then becoming meaningless and boring again. The play started without me. (This was a relief.) I crept around the corner into the hall and stood in the aisle, near the door, to watch.

My eyes were on the two surviving kings. I wanted to see how my absence changed the play (not much) and I wanted to catch Ash's eye so that I could pull a face and then he would like me again. I wanted to be able to kick somebody and still to be liked by the person I had kicked. That was normal if not excusable, it was a fundamental principle of class and race relations in the whole country at the time. Meanwhile the music started, and in the foreground a fuchsia-pink figure jumped down from the stage.

Delilah landed in front of somebody's father. I don't know whose he was but he was a big man, red-faced and wax-jacketed. Delilah leaned forward over him and the empty bust of her dress hung open to reveal a ten-year-old boy's red nipples. Everyone laughed. But at the same moment we could see that something was happening to this man. His face took on a swollen look and his lips tightened together, as though he was suppressing his breath. Delilah flipped the man's tie over his shoulder and moved on. She ignored the person in the next seat, a woman, and perched herself on the next adult male in the row. As she settled in his lap her eyes widened in exaggerated shock, as though she had encountered something unexpected, and she jumped up again at once and waggled her finger in the father's face.

This man reached out and grabbed Delilah by the shoulder, swung his arm around her and put his hand right over her mouth. There was a sound of concern from the people who were sitting nearby, which seemed to wake the man up. He loosened his grip, Delilah slipped from his grasp, winked at him, and carried on as though it was an intentional part of her performance. In the back rows, people were standing up so that they could get a better view. Delilah worked her way along the front row, perching on each male lap in her path, inviting the fathers, uncles, and grandfathers to fondle her flat chest or run their hands up her thighs toward the place where the fuchsia dress bulged, just a little bit, and they dazedly did it in front of everybody. Nobody intervened. A trancelike feeling settled over me. Mrs. Hepton banged out the tune on the piano and Delilah sang her solo tunelessly and perfectly. The audience, in the hall and onstage, shrieked.

Stu's birthday party was in late summer. I went alone, and it was on my way home that I got lost. I left the path and cut through the undergrowth, where the wood was full of tall and plain plants, long stalks and tough leaves, growing densely among one another. The plants had expertly intermeshed themselves to catch the light, tender offshoots branching horizontally in the spaces between one another like interlaced fingers. They created a cryptic tangle, I couldn't see farther than a few paces in any direction, or rather, I could see—I could see the plants, who were proud. Not one shrank back. Each accepted what it needed and took its place. As a collective, they held tall, each one focused on its own optimal survival, but they weren't fighting. They didn't have any use for distinctions between the beautiful and the critical. Everywhere I looked, every single thing was up to something. I heard a vehicle approaching and realized that I was right at the edge of the wood, near the road. I staggered toward the sound, and emerged to see a police car swish past. It was traveling fast, without lights or siren, and I could see that the direction I was facing in was the wrong one—not into the village but toward the flower farm. When I saw the car turn down the lane, away from the main road, I knew the whole story, which appeared suddenly and with clarity before me, as though I was rounding a corner and a wide new prospect had come into view. The men who worked on the flower farm never used to come into the village. That single occasion, mushrooming, was the only time I had come close to them. Suddenly their absence was glaring. I stood at the edge of the wood and looked over to the flower farm, the sunflowers browning in the field, and watched the car beetling along the drive and pulling up in front of the house.

The case did not come out for some time after that. National news reported on the agency, which connected men from Bulgaria and Romania with employers in England. They knew how to find vulnerable or isolated individuals whose absence wouldn't be missed—ex-prisoners, people with learning difficulties, addicts, and young people who had grown up in care. The two women who ran the agency took possession of the passports of these men and, while they were working, used their identities to take out loans.

Only the local paper was interested in the individual workers and the flower farmer. On a national scale, he was just one of the many employers who ran farms, shops, car washes, cafés, and cleaning companies, who had worked in partnership with this agency, and his crimes were not the most heinous. The farmer had completed pay stubs which did not reflect the hours his employees had worked. He charged them for accommodation in his caravans, which had broken doors and windows; mold on the walls, curtains, and windows; no smoke detectors; a leaking waste tank which caused the floor in one to collapse; and, at times, no running water—the men had been washing in the river. The men worked sixty-hour weeks, one had worked for eighteen consecutive days. These details were all published. This went on until, almost by chance, on a farm in Lincolnshire, another of this agency's workers hailed a police car that happened to pass him as he walked along a deserted rural road.

The flower farmer escaped with a light sentence. The reason for this was that there were only two workers on his farm at the time the arrests were made and only one of these men was willing to provide evidence against him. I heard that the other worker was scared of repercussions, and also that he had severe learning difficulties which prevented him from taking the stand, and also that he had been quietly disappeared. Then the local newspaper tracked him down to a salmon farm in provincial Sofia and found something quite different. The man was willing to make public the account he had given the police. He said that he had no problem with the work. His caravan had the utilities he needed and he accepted that he would pay for his accommodation. He told the press that it was English employment law that was the problem. Couldn't English people choose when, and for how long, they wanted to work? Personally, he preferred to work long hours, many days in succession, and then return to his wife after only a few months away. Otherwise he would have had to work away from home for most of the year. The couple had no children and his wife was lonely when he went. They were only recently married.

I watched the police car stop outside the farmhouse but I didn't stay to give it sustained attention because it would take a long time to walk back to my house. When, eventually, I got home, there were two women sitting at the kitchen table. Two small glass beakers of green wine. A used tin for an ashtray. A large, square hardback book in shiny covers, closed on the table between them.

My mother was in her work clothing. Across from her, the blond girl in a faded blue-grey-purple dress narrowed her eyes, scrutinizing me, as she pulled a licorice-colored cigarette paper out of the packet. "Do you remember me?"

"Serena."

Serena smiled. "Good work, last time you thought I was Teresa."

"You haven't got a tan."

She licked the paper. "It wasn't hot where I went."

"But you have been away."

She nodded.

"Can I please have my present?" I said.

My mother said my name in a reproving way. Serena reached under the table, into her backpack, and drew out a slim oblong of dark purple tissue paper. I held it for a moment and felt its light, mysterious form.

"How was your trip?" I asked.

"It was a total disaster," she said, "but I've got a new job."

I waited. She pulled on her cigarette. "There's a British Council office in Taipei."

This didn't mean much to me. I looked to my mother, who said, "Shall we visit?"

I shrugged. "Yep."

"Open it," said Serena.

Inside the purple tissue there was a small, flat woman made out of an oval piece of wood smoothed to silkiness. The wood had a faintly spicy smell. The woman was painted onto the wood with a brush as fine as a thorn. Her body was wrapped in clothing in shades of sage and jade. Her eyes were two liquid lines and her black hair in a topknot was a tumbling crest like a midnight wave. From the side of her skirt issued strange pointed teeth, no space between them, as fine as wooden needles. She was a comb.

"I wish you could have seen the woman who made them," said Serena. "It was all waste wood, old furniture, boxes, broken branches. She'd bring a new one out of a chunk in any shape in the time it takes to smoke a cigarette." She put the cigarette in her mouth and twirled her hands.

My mother frowned, just slightly. She rose and started to clear clean dishes from the sink. I held the comb in my flat palm. It was the length of my hand, from wrist to fingertip. "Yours is cedar," said Serena.

"Have a look at my book," my mother said over her shoulder.

I flipped the cover on the huge book on the table and it fell open at the center: a color image, a double-page spread. A photographic reproduction of a large piece of old paper. Most of this paper was washed in a pale grey-blue-purple color that had been painted, mistily, across the background.

A small portion of this large piece of paper carried a painted landscape, seen from a distance. There were mountains and trees. A stream became powerful as it forced its way through rocks. Nestled in the background hills there was a tiny turreted building. A blue-purple-grey background, the color of Serena's dress, ran through every bit of the picture. It faded across the rocks in the foreground and swept through the branches of the trees, moved in the water, and highlighted the walls of the buildings. The building itself was small, only one detail of the background. It looked cozy, nestled in its landscape. The trees were inked equally finely. When I looked carefully I could see an alder and a willow. And another smaller, bent alder. "Made in China," I said, and Serena nodded seriously.

We had chicken for dinner. My parents told Serena about our plans to move into the city (they had proper jobs and had found a terraced house available to rent) and I tuned out, sinking into my own private narratives in the way that only children teach themselves to do. Then my mother was saying something which seized my attention: ". . . and I was about eight, a dog in the park jumped on me and pinned me down, I still have dreams about looking up into its jaws hanging open. The owner said that he was only trying to play."

I remembered it too. For a moment I was convinced that the memory had been transmitted to me like a heritable disease, but I was old enough to know better. Something similar must have happened to me, a long time ago, or else she had told it to me before. I have to remind myself that I can't see into other people's thoughts or memories or interior lives.

Yesterday, in the early evening, all the doors were open inside the apartment opposite and I could see light pouring through the wide west-facing window at the other side of their building and against it, cardiganed back turned to me, was the woman at her sewing machine. She'd moved to another room. I can't help thinking that she moved to avoid me, that she didn't want to catch my eye every time she glanced up from her work, or when we were both up in the early hours. More likely her reasons had nothing to do with me. I'm glad I was wrong about her having the virus. My window box, facing the window where she used to work, is suffering now. The plants are clustered with aphids. At first I thought they needed watering, then I thought they were overwatered, and it was only after several days, leaves curling and stalks bending, that I looked closely enough to see the aphids, whitish rather than green, filling out every fine line on each plant. It took several days more to notice that the ants were hurrying up and down the stalks, herding the aphids. The ants farm and eat the aphids and the aphids consume my plants, which look grim. I have decided to choose the plants over the aphids, over the ants. I bought a packet of nematode worms from a Dutch supplier online, they're microscopic—it looks like a plastic sachet of dust, with instructions to sprinkle it on the earth surrounding the plants. The nematodes exude a scent or hormone that the ants can't stand, and so they can't bear to be within ten meters of the nematodes. That way I can get the ants out of our space without killing them. I can wash off the aphids with soapy water.

Serena stayed for a whole week. At the weekend my parents went out and she played with me, real games involving running, I had a glimpse of what it would be like to be a sibling. When I'd caught her several times she stretched out on the grass, face down, and told me that she was very, very old. "Can I rest? We could bake something."

I sat down beside her and nodded. "I know how to do that."

We found flour, a piece of ginger, and black molasses. We walked to the shop for eggs and made it just in time before Mr. Colvin closed for lunch. "From the ladies next door," he said—he meant Mr. Gray's hens.

At home I sieved the flour and ground ginger and bicarbonate of soda into a bowl, peppering the table with pale powder, like the corona of an eclipse, around the shape of the bowl. Serena didn't tell me to be careful. She warmed the black treacle and butter together in a copper pan over a small blue flame. When I had made a grainy mountain in my bowl I made a well with my hands, but it was so silky that I could hardly feel my fingertips. I cracked the egg into the crater and poured in some milk. At first it was a mess, lumpy and dry, but it only took a few stirs for it to come together in the form of a smooth galaxy inside the bowl. I instructed Serena to pour in the black liquid, little by little, until it was evenly dark, and, cautiously, we spilled the mixture into the tin, slid the tin into the oven.

The smell of the unmade cake pulled physically on something inside me and I told Serena that we needed to lick the bowl. We scraped the wet mixture off the sides with blunt knives and licked it off the blade.

When the cake had been in for half an hour, we took it out and put a clean blade into the center. The blade came out covered in dragging brown lines of wet mixture.

We put it back in, and brought it out again ten minutes later. The edges of the cake were rising and turning dark and treacly, just on the edge of crisp, but the knife still came out of the center clotted with damp crumbs. Serena picked up the hot tin with a dish towel and shoved it back in the oven. She kicked the metal door closed and it slammed with a cracking sound.

"It will be raw in the middle and burnt on the outside," she said angrily. "I can't do things like this." But we turned off the heat and the cake rested in the cooling oven, I thought it was fine when it came out.

After Serena had left, and the final third of the cake was turning stale in a box in the kitchen, it occurred to me to place a piece of it on

the wall behind Alice's house, but I didn't because I was too reasonable. Alice was long gone. The deer, surely, too. I did walk past
Alice's house, which I hadn't done so much since she had moved out,
even less so after Soldier died and I could take a direct route home
from the school bus stop. The building had been made into a holiday
rental and looked good for it, the doors and window frames had
been painted olive green and there was a pot of white lavender by
the door, the flowers turning brown but not yet cut back. Somehow,
as the developer, builder, and renovator had passed in and out, the
ash tree by the wall had evaded chain saws. It was still standing, still
perilously dangling its blackened branches over the road. At the
base of the wall, on the verge, it had a tentacular base, like claws
running into the earth. The trunk, up close, was surfaced with a net-
like pattern of grooves which parted in repeating diamonds,
mapping the area across which it had outgrown itself. The lines
made shallow ravines, some of which had moisture trickling down
them, so that they looked like a river delta. It was a damp day. I
looked behind me, across bare brown fields to the edge of the wood.
The sky was intense, with rust- and purple-colored clouds through
which amber sunlight was somehow escaping. Low-slanting light
shone on a huge beech tree on the edge of the wood and the tree, lit
as though by a powerful lamp, stood radiant against the deep sky,
brown and yellow leaves like coins clinging on. I turned back and
the trunk of the ash was close to my face. The very outer surface of the
wood was green and powdery with a moss whose bright dry grains
looked bushy up close, like a rainforest seen from above. Patches of
grey lichen splotched the trunk, each one with ragged edges like a
coastline. On the farmyard side, the rotting wood was much darker,
with bright orange and tiny white pinpricks on it, like a city at night

seen from an airplane. A cluster of pearly mushrooms was growing out of a deep crack, spreading upward from the hollow at the base. Where the wood parted it was slick to touch.

Along the front of the trunk, where the wood was green and brown and dry, there was a bulging uneven line. Within this line a metal wire was apparent, in places. The tree trunk had grown and closed over it elsewhere, so the horizontal line made the image of a braced or gagged mouth. The wire, strung through the wall where it was collapsing, had been run across the outer edge of the tree. The tree had grown into and over it, at its own pace, swollen and healed around it. I tapped. The wood here was sound. The living branch was still growing strong. It had thickened. Small branches were radiating from its base and upward. Though this living part was stunted by growing against the thick, partly dead trunk, the form that it was taking was no longer that of a large branch, but that of a small tree.

One day my mother collected me in the car from school. She had been working nearby. I was embarrassed by her car's broken exhaust, and ashamed of my embarrassment. I was quiet on the way home. She drove slowly as she always did. As we approached the racehorse stables she asked me whether I knew that Clare had been in the hospital again and I said that I did.

"Sadly," my mother said carefully, "Clare caught an infection while she was very weak."

"Oh," I said. I turned to look at my mother, who kept her eyes on the road. "So is she dead?"

Clare had hair and she had started secondary school. Her death had been present beside her through childhood—but when this went on, and on again, and on for months and years, I think we all had stopped expecting it, and we lived in the knowledge of the inevitability of her death but no real expectation of it. Her illness and fragility was a feature of her character.

"Yes," said my mother.

Out of the window I could see three small black ponies in a field. They were stocky and shiny with frizzy manes. They were running very fast together around the perimeter fence, and then suddenly they slowed down, and then they started to gallop again. I asked why Clare had died.

"She had an infection from a tiny fungus that is present everywhere, in bins and compost heaps or damp in a house. We all have it inside our bodies all the time. When a person is very weak it can be dangerous." I cut her off—"I already know about that."

We drove on for a while and reached the crossroads. My mother stopped to look both ways, as she always did, even though this road was always clear.

"Perhaps that isn't what you meant," she said. "Well, there are things that could have happened to Clare which make her more likely to be poorly in the way that she was. Things in the air and food and medicines, X-Rays before you are born." Her voice got louder as though she was expressing growing certainty. "It runs in families. It's to do with poverty and that's a complex problem. It's not easy to explain. Some people call it bad luck but I wouldn't."

It was a spring day, months later, when I looked over the edge of the quarry and I noticed a space in the side where the wall had fallen away. I saw the vole in there and he ran up and out into the grass. A kestrel rose above him. I stood waiting to see who would make the first move. And then I noticed that the quarry had begun to fill with water again.

When I saw the water I gave back the space to the hawk and the vole. I backed away and ran to the house that used to be Clare's. Maybe because I was thinking about the rabbits, maybe because I was used to retracing my footsteps, following the same paths, maybe just because Clare's family lived nearer the quarry than anybody else.

Nic was sitting on the step with a mug beside her, looking out. I stopped in front of her and felt a moment's shyness again. The moment before you walk into a party, alone, and you wish you could go home. It was impossible to go back. Nic had seen me.

She looked the same as she always had. I stopped in front of her.

"There's water in the quarry again," I said.

"I can see that," said Nic.

When I turned to look over my shoulder, to follow her gaze, I could see that she could see right down and over the quarry from her position on the step. She would have watched the first flooding from there when Adam was small and Clare had just started school. She would have seen the new machinery go in and drain the quarry and line it while Dmitri was off on full pay, and then she would have counted through the pounds and the hours measured in the gouges he was directed to make in the bottom and the sides. Now she was watching the water inch up again, beyond control. The bottom of her garden was almost at the quarry's edge. The small pale scar was still there, flattening the edge of her left eye. Her irises were catching the last blaze from the falling light. It amazed me that she hadn't changed in any visible way—as far as I could see. In every interaction I watched her closely and I listened carefully. I came away with nothing. That day I asked her if Adam was playing and she told me to go on in.

Adam and I used to walk around the edge of the houses, along the high wall above Thomas Gray's small field, down the steep hill running into the village on the opposite side to our homes. The trees grew tall on one side, and there was a high wall on the other, so you couldn't see far inside its tunnel. Empty quarry trucks used to speed past there toward the site, making the grass flatten back against the verge and flustering the sycamores. On the way back, loaded and running uphill, the trucks moved at a statelier pace. From the high wall I could see into the yard outside the Gray farm and I had to admit that it was true, what Mr. Gray was insisting on. Sometimes the security light over his yard was lighting up during the day, when nobody was there. Mr. Gray had become paranoid about this. He thought he had a ghost. I thought that whatever had happened to his mother's mind was coming early to his. The ghost thing seemed unlikely to me—the barn was a new build. But I also noticed the lighting issue. From across the landscape, standing on the wall, Adam and I could see the lights flicking on and off in daylight.

The barn stood close to the public road. Inside there were bright strip lights above the cattle stalls, and outside there was a security light which illuminated Mr. Gray's small collection of uninsured vehicles which he used on the farm. Both lights were accessible from a switch by the door inside the barn. I suggested to Mr. Gray that it was people like myself—young and bored people—coming in off the road for something to do, but he shook his head and said that he would see them going in and out. I had to agree.

I requested to feed the cattle in the mornings that winter. I had a feeling that there would be something useful to me in spending my time with their calm presence in their orderly space. Mr. Gray agreed. Often, when I went in in the mornings, the interior lights were already on. Once, when I knocked half a bale onto the floor and it poofed open with a soft explosion, the burst of dust rose up into the air and a black rag dislodged itself from the rafters. It came flying at my head. I felt its breeze over my hair and I ducked, but it spun past me, hissing. A bat. It veered and disappeared through the open door, into the blue hour of morning. Through the door the slopes of the buildings, vehicles, and hills were surfaced with frost. Midwinter outside—the bat was going out to its death. I told Mr. Gray about it and Mr. Gray took out the bulbs from inside the barn, saying that the ghost was disrupting the cattle's rhythms. He disconnected the sensor on the security light. Still, that light went on and off. If one of us went in there was nobody there.

On my way out one frosty morning the sun was melting a slick of snow on all the surfaces. I could see the tops of the trees behind the house in front of which the distance arose in cold and sunlit space, luminously empty. Then the emptiness was suffused by a scrabbling sound. On the front of the rusted white Land Rover a small rook, some fluff among its plumage, was falling down the icy windshield. It rolled right over, legs in the air, tumbling over its back and front and back and then landing safely on its feet on the flat of the hood. It shook itself off. I held my breath to prevent the steam from billowing out of my mouth. The small rook sidestepped and fluttered back to the top of the windshield, where another young rook was standing, poised. They descended together this time, scrabbling and tumbling, just beyond safety or control, onto the hood, where they collapsed into one form, then separated and collected themselves, all without squawking. On the roof of the vehicle there was another rook, an adult, who seemed to have no interest in what the two youths were doing. She stood with her short legs wide apart and her wings hunched, preening. I could hear the faint clipping sound of her beak nibbling at the root of her feathers. I had an urge to clap my hands to make them all fly off. On the windshield their feathers had melted the frost in dappled patterns, beneath which the frost traced feather shapes.

I caught the light culprit inside the barn in early spring. Ivy. One morning when I went in to feed she was there, in the act, stretching her neck out so long, long so that she did not look like a cow anymore, long, long over the barrier at the wall toward the door, she pressed the switch with her nose. On. Off.

I ran to tell Mr. Gray.

"Ivy's dead," he said. I told him to come and look.

Ivy hid herself behind her family, near the back wall, when we came in. She lowered her head to the ground where she had a view of what we were doing. I saw the glint of her eye between the others' legs. When I pointed it out Mr. Gray looked grim. "That's her daughter," he said. "Lucy."

Lucy was separated from the rest of the herd and gated away from the light switches. In spring she was moved with her young son to the field on the side of the road out of the village, the field below the wall that Adam and I had made our base. It must have been an old field: small. When I sat on that wall with Adam, Lucy and her son came up and nosed our feet. Always Lucy came first and her son followed after she had established that the situation was safe. She appeared inside that field again the next summer, her son, now a bullock, with her again. I suspected Mr. Gray of sentimentality in giving her a companion. The closeness of mother and son was obvious, even to a human. They were more completely attached than any other parent and child I have ever known. They never moved more than a few meters from one another and they were always doing the same thing—grazing, or lying down, or standing, tails flicking in the heat. Once or twice I saw them resting their heads together along the shoulders, as horses do. It appeared to me as a loving friendship but perhaps this was a projection of my own emotion, it's equally possible that their quiet connection was grief, and their experience was that of being the only survivors of their species, occasionally hearing the ghostly voice of another of their kind on the wind. I grew used to seeing the two of them together there. Then one day Lucy was lying down with her four stiff legs at an angle from the ground, pointing diagonally toward the sky, and her body hugely swollen.

I ran to the farm and Mr. Gray came out right away. "Oh," he said. One hand rose to smooth his eyebrow with quick nervous sweeping motions. "Lucy?"

Behind him, inside the house, something moved. Cat's face appeared, resting her chin on Mr. Gray's shoulder. She looked strange, very pale, as though the life force had been rinsed out of her. I must have been staring because she grinned and said: "No makeup."

Mr. Gray walked on ahead of us. Cat said that she didn't have any boots and Mr. Gray did not seem to hear. She put on a pair of his, complaining that his feet were too big, and he ignored her and walked on up ahead.

We went in silence to the field, Cat's feet slopping inside the boots. I kept pace with her, casting sideways glances at her strange face. It was the eyelashes: they were thick and very long, but white-blond like her hair. She looked alien. I liked it.

I could see the bullock standing over his mother. There was a magpie at her eye. Mr. Gray arrived at the body first. "Bloat," he said. "I should have put a lick out."

"What's that?"

Cat was pointing at the head. There was a small, perfectly round red puncture with a thick line of blood like black jam coming out of it. Bang in the middle of Lucy's forehead. There was something odd about the shape: it was too symmetrical, too regular. Mr. Gray shrugged evasively. "Crows."

Cat laughed. "Are you serious?" She squinted at him, her forehead creased, and then reached out to touch him between the eyes, at precisely the place where Lucy had a wound, with her middle finger. She pressed harder and harder until he had to lean back and bat her hand away.

"Bang," she said.

Mr. Gray turned to me. "Did you know that Catherine is abandoning public service?"

Cat also addressed me. "They're closing the fire station."

"Who are?"

She shrugged. "I told them, I can't commute an hour into town every day. So I've got a job on a rig."

"You?" I said.

Cat winked at me. "Ten men to every girl."

"It's not a real place," said Mr. Gray. "They don't abide by law. Look at the Green boy who lost his hand."

"Fingers," I said. Everybody knew that he still had the thumb.

"Exactly," said Mr. Gray. "What will he farm with now?"

I didn't respond and neither did Cat. In the quiet, the still body in front of me recalled my attention, and hers, and, eventually,

Mr. Gray's. When Cat broke the silence her voice was soft and serious. "You would be in trouble for this."

Mr. Gray made a gently derisive sound. "What do you think
happens to the rest of them?"

Cat shook her head, still grave. "This is singling out."

"She'd taught herself how to open the gate," he said.

I felt cold air run through me and I looked up at Mr. Gray, who
looked back at me kindly. "I can't say I'm sorry to have got rid of her."

The pale hairs on the cow's belly were dispersed over the tight
swollen skin. A little earth was packed into the ridges on her hooves.
Her son stood beside her with huge patience. His ears were low and
his tail flicking mindlessly. The smell of her body, as yet weak, infil-
trated my body. Flies were busy landing and taking off around the
reservoir of her tear duct. Mr. Gray broke the silence to complain
about the cost of calling out the knacker. Later that year he pulled
up the hedges in that small field so that it became a corner of the
larger field behind it, which he rented out to another farmer. For a
while I could still see the lines where the hedge used to be, then the
tenant ploughed it up and reseeded it because the grass was poor.
The ground turned on its head and the wind flowed across this bare
brown skin all autumn. I guess he had no use for a very small field
anymore. I never saw Cat after that.

Adam and I found a five-pound note on the road at the edge of
that field. The wind picked up the money from the dust on the verge
and lifted it to our eyes, then dropped it at our feet, like a carnivore
playing with its prey. We spotted it at exactly the same time. Neither
of us were certain of its value. We stood in the middle of the road for
a while, taking it in turns to hold it. It was dry, old, paper money. It
had, I think, been through the wash: a little bit furry. I thought of my

vole and the baby rabbits. Fine elastic skin under down. A truck approached and Adam and I scrambled up the steep shoulder. Adam said that he wanted to take the money to his mother. He said that she would split it for us and that my mother would most likely make us *give it back* somewhere. I nodded. There was nowhere to return it.

Nic's kitchen was warm and steamy. Everything was on: the kettle, the television on the counter, a pan with peeled potatoes boiling in it, and the washing machine. When she saw me, she apologized for the state of it and said that she would have cleaned up if she'd known we were on our way in. This brought tears to my eyes and I concealed them, successfully, I think. Adam showed her the five-pound note and she took out her purse. It was large, warm, soft, and brown. It opened with a golden clip which made a satisfying noise. Nic folded the note carefully into the purse and she took out two coins. In exchange for the five-pound note, she gave one pound to both of us.

Adam was too young to see the difference in quantity but I understood. I took the money and I felt that the transaction realigned something which had fallen out of sync for me. Everywhere people went on and on about taking it in turns, lining up, sharing, and fairness, but these obligations, forced onto children, were not what I observed in the world. The equality that had been preached at me had hardly been a part of the reality that I had experienced. In Nic's house, I imagined, even less so. A pound was a lot of money for me and for Adam so it was a reasonable exchange.

I knew where I would spend it. Once a week I went with my mother to the big shop, Safeway. That week I took my money. I knew its destination: the thing I always wanted was the white sliced bread.

The supermarket was brightly lit and quiet. Automatic doors opened and raked us with chilly air as we went in. I left my mother in the vegetable aisle looking at the ranks of root vegetables which had been selected, ordered, and configured for conformity, like army boys. Identical forms terrified me. Some of the species had traveled a few miles, from the fields outside the town. Others had come from the other side of the world. They all lay together, divided by thin wooden partitions so that the coriander from India wouldn't tumble into the carrots from West Yorks. I was not concerned with this vegetal zone and I wandered off, along the long alleyway which ran along the aisles' end, past an unmanned meat counter and a rack of hardening baguettes. I was looking for long-life bread. I had my coin in my fist. I found the bread and identified the thing I wanted: a loaf with a picture of a smiling and very Aryan boy on the front. The polyethylene bag and the bread beneath it were almost formless, a cloud in my hands. Then I studied the rest of the aisle. Doughnuts, cakes in plastic boxes, snack bars, cardboard boxes of cereal that had escaped the fields and had been translated into astronauts and cartoon animals. There was nothing alive inside this building, except humans. That was why it was safe.

A young man in a peaked hat appeared at the end of the aisle, loped toward me, and crouched down so that our faces were level.

"Are you on your own in here?"

My mother did not trust authority and had always told me to stay silent, if captured, and never to confess anything. In silence I led the man to the end of the aisle and retraced my footsteps toward the vegetables. My mother wasn't there. The man and I walked back, all the way to the alcohol at the far end of the shop, but each aisle was empty. We went to the registers and asked the people whether they had seen anybody fitting my mother's description and they had not.

Slowly, grain by grain, I felt my acute and intense desire for the products exchange itself for a low and chronic need for my mother. We passed the biscuits with cream sandwiched between them, we passed the ring-shaped crisps, we passed the freezers stacked with oily ice-cream cake with layers of mint, vanilla, and dark chocolate and I felt a total lack of desire. The slippery-floored aisles were empty. I did not cry, however; I noticed that each time I breathed in, the inhalation was attended by a low-pitched noise. I knew that I should not explain to the man that I was asthmatic. He took me outside and we stood beside the door. He patted my shoulder. By the way he held his arm, stiffly at an angle, and by the way he set his mouth, I could see that he didn't feel comfortable touching me. In fact, he needed me to know that he wasn't enjoying himself when he patted me. That was when I noticed that he was a real person who also came out of a body and had a home to go to and it was the first time I had a sense of somebody else's mind, with me in its foreground, wandering all around us, toward the clock which announced that his break was due, the steak bake on top of the microwave in the staff kitchen, his auntie's steak and chips, his auntie's incontinent puppy, his auntie's stent, dogsitting, his new trainers, his girlfriend's giggling, driving with the windows open all winter. Dog hair on the back seat. An outside world projected on the inside. My breathing cleared and slowed, my airways opened up, my body calmed down. I pulled on the man's arm. "She's over there."

When I climbed back into the car I still had my coin in my fist, which had taken on a metallic smell. The coin, now as warm as my body, had dodged its fate: it should have been lying in the super-market register in a gridded plastic tray, on the next stop on a fitful but inevitable passage toward the capital, where the supermarket was headquartered, where the banks were headquartered, and where, sooner or later, my coin would vanish into pixels like the coins that Mario and Luigi absorb into their bodies with a plinking sound. My coin would take up a new, virtual existence as a digit on a screen, its body disappeared, its soul residing with virtual mountains of virtual coins inside a massive virtual pocket whose capacity to hold money grows and grows, without geographical space expanding by an inch. Money loves to follow the same routes to the same destinations, natural as water falling out of a spring. This was in the lead-up to the millennium, when there was a vogue for time capsules containing solid objects. Later, at home, I buried my gold coin with the thought that somebody might find it in another geological epoch. I wanted to take it out of circulation. The ground it was buried in was, itself, falling out of circulation, into a gap between a city and the sea, somewhere outside the story of progress or history, falling between center and margin, power and powerless, exploiter and victim, dis-balanced and uneven. The tentacles of the place extended across the entire planet and it was a little local cluster of cottages. In spite of the Forestry Commission, the agribusinesses, and the quarry, it was not industrial. It wasn't pastoral, in spite of the meadows and the herds and flocks. I did not know anybody who retailed local folklore or knew the weeds by nicknames, there was no village idiot, no incest, or if there was, I did not know about it because the village was not a close-knit community. People were not much interested in other people's business, there was no more curtain-twitching than there was in the urban neighborhoods in which I have lived. Personally, I was usually more interested in the television than in my real neighbors. I used to come in from playing out every day at 5:35 because it was time to watch a program about a neighborhood on the other side of the planet and the atmosphere of this neighborhood was continuous with the place in which I lived, a quiet summer morning in suburban Melbourne, the whirring of the birds, gentle post-dawn light trickling through slim, pale eucalyptus leaves, cars quiet in their private bays gradually emerging from the shadows that drain away around them, water through sand, and then on the same screen a few minutes later the warm night comes down with a chorus of crickets and the eucalyptus trees filtering white light from streetlamps, shadows taking back the forms of things into the shapeless dark with its spray of stars, inset within a cold late autumn afternoon in the northern hemisphere where the apples are rotting in the grass, feverfew is coming up in tussocks in the neglected corners of the empty wheat field where the mud is purplish, the leaves on the cherry trees are turning through the colors at the point of a flame, the defoliated hedges are thickened with mist between the twigs and lipstick-pink spindle berries, the pale blue sky turns dark, the dregs of the sunset are drained off, and, on the other side of the horizon, the glow of sodium from the freeway intensifies. At ten to six the sound of a car with a broken exhaust interrupts the soundtrack and parks up outside the house. (A parent, arriving home.) The soap operas were nested inside the television, beside the books on the shelves which enclosed yet other worlds. My mother, who may have been thinking that my experience was narrow, had quietly been putting in my way stories from different times and places—brothers who lived in a low-rise block in Brixton, a princess who lived in a castle in medieval Flanders, a young warrior in a rainforest in precolonial

Nicaragua, a girl in an electric wheelchair in a fishing port in Japan. Few of these books were written by people who had the authority of experience—the authors didn't really know what they were talking about—and so they did not deliver these wider worlds into my environment with anything like fullness. Still, they gave me a knowledge that the other worlds were there and that they had volume in a universe of provincial lives, in the way that glowworms made the space inside the forest appear.

IT WAS LATE IN THE year, a weekday. We had not yet broken up but there was a training day at school and I was bored. The windows in the village were dull in daytime like switched-off screens. Where was everybody? This was no place to be alive. In somebody's front garden, even the lemon-colored dahlias were ruined, bent, soft and heavy with age and rain. Wet trickled on the tree trunks and house fronts. I walked to the graveyard and looked at the names, righted some plastic flowers.

I walked out to the hill where the bus had rolled down. On the other side of the valley the larches were revealing themselves in the plantation—it was all similar needly trees but the larches, which had been planted in a zigzag line, weren't evergreen and so they highlighted themselves in yellow at this time of year. In summer I couldn't see the difference. At the entrance to the wood a muckheap had recently been removed to be spread out on the field, leaving behind it a large oval of stinking black liquid, marbled with gasoline rainbows. Inside the wood leaf-fall was thick on the track, sycamore leaves with black spots and entirely black ash. There were piles of long, felled logs but they had been there for a long time. Fragile mushrooms grew out of the gaps and the bark was peeling away in the wet like flesh coming away from bone. A few logs had a measurement across their diameter daubed on in neon-orange paint. In the ditch below them there were brown rotting stalks, horsetail ferns, spiky dark green reeds whose interiors were full of foam. Looking down into it I skidded and fell over. I picked myself up. The track slipped away beneath me in yellow clay. Another foot had slid in the same place. It was a huge footprint made by a chunky boot. The print was perfect, rays around the edge of the sole and tiny crosses at the center. I had assumed that I would turn back and go home here, at the place where the track became impassable, but somebody had repaired it. The boggy trenches had been filled with broken pottery and I recognized it, bottle-green tiles and other shards with brown, cream, navy-blue patterns. The china clay crunched under my feet.

At the center of the wood three huge, ancient yew trees stood at the side of the track. This was as far as you could get from the public road. The yew area had the feel of an island, a distinct ecosystem rising out of a sea, because the trees were larger, more squat, and darker than the deciduous trees which were planted in lines, which were long and thin and only had branches right at the top. The yew branches went low, one dipped to create a huge bench. Another tree had come up and toppled over, exposing a circular, sandy plate of roots the size of a tractor. I paused to look at it when something squawked above me.

It wasn't a bird but a thickset tortoiseshell cat, lying like a jaguar full-length along a branch. She jumped neatly down into a hollow created by the uprooted tree. I couldn't see inside and didn't draw her out. I'd been told that feral animals are vicious—the combination of wildness and civilization creates perverted beings. It wasn't that we were all nudging and adapting to one another all the time. I left her there and went on round the loop.

It was quiet. Light rain went through the leaves. It came in swells, breathily, and I walked in the middle of the path to avoid the cascade of droplets that came down in curtains with every surge. When I looked up I could see birds flitting away as I approached, like debris rippling outward from an explosion. Suddenly, the trees parted and the view opened out. I could see that the forest was advancing out over the edge of the field. In spring, when I came back, the young trees were distinguishable by their leaves. Birch, elder, and buddleia grew out of the side of the quarry. These gaps used to be the burrows in which the sand martins lived but the sand martins didn't come again after the spring the Canadians drained the quarry. In their place, these small trees. Without the martins the quarry was no longer the same place. The dry base meant that there were fewer bugs, therefore fewer martins, therefore fewer predators, therefore I rarely went there to look at the view. Where the wood petered out above the quarry there was an area of cleared scrubby land, empty and brown when I first entered it, but when I sat there patiently for a space of time I could see earwigs and woodlice. An ash leaf heaved into motion and was sucked down by a glistening pink mitten that was curled around its tip, hauling downward, reverse quarrying. The brown of the ash leaves was paler than the rich brown of the soil, which was more consistent than the marbled browns, yellows, oranges, and blacks of a decaying piece of wood which was warm to my touch. I lay down next to it. With my eyes below grass level I noticed that there was a tiny forest down there. My shins went higher than the tops of its highest trees. A bright red stalk, two inches high, with a sycamore leaf pushing out of the top. At the edge of a half-grown beech thicket, below an empty nest, there were four tiny cherry trees and several more cherry stones in bird shit, rotting. A small, elegant oak already had a bunch of cloud-shaped leaves. No conservationist would be able to define this collection of tiny trees as a forest; it is easier to protect the past than the future. Running between all these trees and through spears of the wild grasses there were transparent threads, connecting each one to all the others. When they came into focus they were everywhere. I could see the path where I had walked in, along which the cobwebs were torn apart. Each broken thread terminated at the point where it had broken, where it had stretched, stretched, and then snapped. On either side of the breaking point the two new ends, overstretched, had curled back on themselves. These sections of thread, attached at one side to the stalk or the ground, rose up at the broken end so that they looked like so many limbs, tiny hooks at the top, waving back at me from the places where my knee had snagged them, marking a path through the grass. The ends were sticky, some of them had already attached themselves to other threads or moorings, others made new connections as I watched. Their action was continuous and not always harmless, they divided as well as drawing together; while threads seemed to embrace one another, others looked like snares. The room around me was being created in these new connections as they were formed and renewed by many minds and mindless forces, and the space itself degraded and vanished when these connections failed. The field stretched out untended in the background, every part full of these involvements which were only visible up close.

In spring, when I saw a group of hares behaving weirdly on the field, I didn't notice these details in the ground beneath their feet.

That was a warm day with moisture in the grass and wind that was warm and wet as breath. The air had a good feeling. Molehills stood up, sticky from rain. There were two hares and their long flat feet were dirty. Their fur looked almost reddish against the muddy grass, it collected the sunlight and glinted. They had their heads down, browsing the grass at some distance from one another. As I watched, one hare pricked up his ears and moved toward the other. She edged away from him and he closed the distance, more aggressively this time. Their synchronized movements gathered speed and he started to chase her. The two bodies bounded heavily over the uneven ground, bouncing up like objects made of solid rubber. At every few paces the female would angle her body in another direction. The male was a little faster than her. As I watched, the space between them disappeared. When the female turned to double back on herself the male was at her shoulder and she spun up in the air and flung herself right over his body in a full revolution. It made me think of ice-skating couples, the female circling above the male head, skirts twinkling.

The female hare landed uphill and took off again, running down the slope. She was running fast for her life and he was closing in behind her. She pushed harder off her back legs, I could see her draw on a new reserve of power and energy. Then, suddenly, she turned to face the male hare and stopped. The male hare stopped too, his movement so attuned that her change was his. The bodies didn't collide or collapse into one. They stood very still. The breeze ruffled his fur like an invisible hand. They faced one another at a whisker's distance. Then they rose up on their legs and began to fight.

The legs they used as arms were short and held quite straight. I could see the wide white bibs on their bellies. The arms were moving so fast that they blurred themselves out. The female toppled right over backward, somersaulted, and rolled up still fighting, but she punched the air—he was just beyond her reach. He caught her face with one heavy blow and then another and she was boxing nothing. She retreated. And then, mid-flight, she turned and started to chase him and he, who had been pursuing her, ran away.

She chased him up the hill, his body zigzagging away from her. They rose, he threw a punch, and then he was chasing her again, and she turned and spun above his body again. They doubled back and turned over onto one another, again, every few paces. It was a confusion. They stopped again and settled back into their own forms. The male was not far from where I was sitting. He sat still behind a tuft of tough grass. I was close enough to see him lick his face. The two hares were both staring into the distance, but it was different distances: she looked toward the road and he looked at me. She moved a little way along the ground, nosing the grass as though no longer interested in her lover or attacker. Then the male turned directly to face her and she spurted off again. They ran a wide circle around the field and when they reached the lower part of the slope another hare appeared.

I did not see the interloper arrive but he ran right into the middle of the field with the energy and purpose of a player subbed on to change the course of the game. He followed the pursuing hare, who turned on his heels and fled. I finally, totally, lost track of which hare was which as the three chased and evaded one another. One hare ran right under the bodies of the others, who hurdled clear in turn. They had all flattened their ears. Two were fighting, one idly nibbling the grass nearby. All three were running a long line, one after the other, and then, doubling back on themselves, they ran in the opposite direction, deleted the line they had traced, the hunter became the hunted. Then, the third hare disappeared, I don't know if it was the original third. Two remained. They had to reveal themselves. One ran up behind the other and climbed onto her back. His pointed face fitted perfectly into the bend of the nape of her neck. She was very still. Then he began to shiver violently and I turned my head aside, out of some sense of respect which meant nothing to them. I had seen a hare's form, it was no more than a dent in the earth; they live their whole lives open to anybody in their surroundings. When I turned back they had separated again, facing in opposite directions, grazing.

Later I was in the same place, it was late summer and I was leaning back into the grasses which had grown tall on the bank and tangled. I realized, as I did so, that I was surrounded by many different tiny wildflowers and that bees were combing them. The flowers were all different colors. Battered faces with purple and green petals. Magenta hairs growing in a green cup. Blue fingers sticking out of a grey stalk.

I lay back in the grass and could see the whole plant, the stalks, stems, pistils, stamens, leaves, and petals, respiring and vibrating, spawning into the surrounding air. Pricks of pollen, particles of scent disseminated. Shrunken and swollen organs bulged. Moisture trickled down the underside of a leaf and a tiny brown bug made its way across a petal and a butterfly landed and stuck in her still-lengthening tongue and the groaning bees entered one flower and then another and another. I watched a striped abdomen disappear inside the pink, purple, yellow, green floral flesh, and when she reappeared her entire body was showered in colored dust. When I started to feel the roots feeling through the earth below my back like cold fingertips through the hair on the back of the head my mind blinked, there was too much going on, but it was drawn back to take its place in the surrounding rampant activity. The moisture dribbled, the insects hovered, fingered, danced, mounted, entered, licked the plants which radiated outward, my eyes and my hair were just one incidental subject of their drenching and luring, every particle excited by every other. The movements were violent and hopelessly desirable, obliterating identities across individuals, species, kingdoms, with each exchange, and every swap was queer and excessively necessary. There was something in the air. I was lying at the foot of the plants and the tall grasses formed high horizons around me so that my whole visible world was a plant world of stalks, insects, earth, sky, water, and light. I could smell not only the green and yellow, sap and honey smells of the plants, but a smell with more depth and past. Its source wasn't visible from the ground. I sat up and looked across the wider landscape. From there I could see black smoke blowing through the hedges and, behind that, the geometric form of a field melting, the stubble illegally on fire, orange flames pouring out of the sides.

At my desk beside the window I could smell real smoke and for a moment I thought that somebody was burning stubble a few miles away and that the wind was carrying it, and then I thought that the smoke was a product of my imagination, but when I sat up straight I could see the flames outside my window. I'd been so absorbed at my screen that I hadn't seen it start, or build. I'd been so busy with my story that I hadn't looked out. My smoke alarm, I realized, was beeping again, but I'd been ignoring that for months. Even now, from where I was sitting, the heat was only a gentle warmth on my skin.

But the homes of my neighbors, in the building opposite, had disappeared inside the blaze.

The smoke moved in many directions, launching into the atmosphere and flowing in a charcoal waterfall out of the windows with one continuous body. The corner of the building, where the wires had run up the side, flamed white-hot. I opened my window and stuck my head out, crushing the recovering geraniums in the window box, and this released their clean spicy smell into the smoke. I could see, on the corner of the street, a gathering of inhabitants. I could make out the woman without her sewing machine, her glasses on a lanyard, holding her cardigan around her, the young parents holding a twin each, and the woman from the top-floor loft, who lives alone. There was even a tropical fish tank balanced inside the double buggy, the water level dangerously low at one end, threatening to slop at the other. The people were all talking to one another, it was the first time I'd seen the different households interacting. Meanwhile the fire explored its surroundings, inflating with each punch of breeze, moving through the earth and air and drawing air and earth inside itself. Red flames dug into the soil and the foundations of the building; pollen specks exploded in the heat; the tree at the side of the block was incandescent, long gold tongues flowing up its trunk and into the branches, pressuring anything living to get out of there.

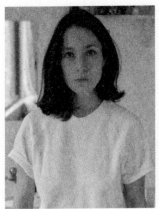

PHOTO BY CALEB KLACES

ABOUT THE AUTHOR

Daisy Hildyard's first novel, *Hunters in the Snow*, received the Somerset Maugham Award and a US National Book Foundation 5 Under 35 honorarium. Her essay *The Second Body*, a brilliantly lucid account of the dissolving boundaries between all life on earth, was published by Fitzcarraldo Editions in 2017. She lives with her family in North Yorkshire, where she was born.